The Army Doctor's Honeymoon Baby

Helen Scott Taylor

Other Books in the Army Doctor's Series

The right of Helen Scott Taylor to be identified as the author of this work has been asserted by her in accordance with the UK Copyright, Designs and Patents Act, 1988.

This is a work of fiction. All the characters in this book have no existence outside the imagination of the author, and have no relation whatsoever to anyone bearing the same name or names. Any resemblance to actual events, locales, or persons, living or dead, is purely coincidental.

Acknowledgments

My thanks to my critique partner Mona Risk for always being there as another set of eyes to check over my story, to my son, Peter Taylor, for creating another lovely book cover, and to Pam Berehulke of Bulletproofing for catching all the little mistakes I missed.

Chapter One

A line of patients stretched out of the hospital and along the ramshackle street of tents and huts that made up the refugee camp near the city of Rejerrah in Africa. Mothers clothed in brightly patterned fabrics waited in line with babies strapped on their backs or chests. The children old enough to walk clung to their mothers' legs or sat playing in the dirt.

In the sweltering heat of the hospital tent, Major Blair Mackenzie wandered between the nurses' stations. He swiped flies away from his face as he stopped to answer a question. It was difficult to focus during the hottest part of the day, but they were short of doctors so he had no time for a break.

A few days earlier a child had been brought in sick with measles. A full-scale vaccination program had started immediately to immunize all children from birth to sixteen. With thirty thousand people living on top of each other in primitive conditions, they were facing a measles epidemic if they didn't act quickly.

A rare and very welcome breeze blew in between the open tent flaps. Blair rubbed his top lip, wiping away sweat and dust. That same dust coated every surface, stung his eyes, gathered in the creases of his skin, and seasoned every meal he ate with a gritty crunch.

He passed behind the nurses from an international

medical charity, all busy giving shots to the children. Although he tried to concentrate, his awareness had skipped ahead to the far side of the hospital tent where Lorna Bell sat. Her blonde hair hung in a braid down her back and her blue T-shirt clung to her curves as she leaned over a tiny infant. She slipped a tape measure around his skinny upper arm to check if he was malnourished.

"Dr. Mac." A young mother cradling her tiny baby in her arms spoke to him.

The Africans in the camp had shortened his name to Mac because they couldn't pronounce Mackenzie. Drawing in a breath, Blair pushed all thoughts of Lorna from his mind and gave the young mother his attention.

She held up her baby. "You put hands on him, Dr. Mac, sir."

Blair pressed his lips together, wanting to refuse. He wished he could debunk this crazy notion the local people had that he was some sort of faith healer. Because he was a pediatrician and his work had improved the mortality rate of children in the camp, they now believed that just by laying his hands on their kids, he could protect them from harm.

He educated families on the risk factors for newborns and young children, but he was a man of science, not a shaman. Try as he might to explain that there was nothing magical about antibiotics and proper nutrition, the nomadic people in the camp didn't believe him.

It was easier to touch the child than stand and argue. He curved his palm beneath the little boy's head and nodded. The pretty young woman gave him a doe-eyed smile, her gaze sliding away shyly before she slipped into the crowd.

Unsettled by this reminder of his near godlike status in the refugee camp, he resumed his path along the busy line of vaccination stations. He answered questions, signed to allow more boxes of vaccine to be distributed, and calmed a man who stormed in because he didn't want his son stuck with a needle.

Finally he reached the end of the row. Lorna glanced up at him from beneath her lashes, a playful sideways look that whisked him back twenty years to their childhood in Scotland. She hadn't changed much and neither had his feelings for her. She was still the only woman who had ever touched his heart.

"Did I see you doing your magical laying on of hands again?" she said.

"I thought you were done teasing me about that."

"Done teasing *you*, Blair Mackenzie?" She cast him another mischievous grin. "Never, laddie."

His heart soared and he grinned back. When he and Lorna bantered, he forgot the heat and dust; he forgot the poverty and sickness that weighed down his heart. Her soft Scottish accent transported him back to his homeland.

All his life, Lorna had been his guiding light. She was a few years his senior. Back when he was a young boy, she'd seemed so much wiser and braver than him. He'd followed her without question, up trees, into caves, out on the boat on the loch, and frequently into trouble with the adults.

When she'd started helping out at a children's charity during her school vacations, he'd been right there at her side and loved every moment of working with the kids. It had been natural for him to specialize in pediatrics when he became a doctor.

Lorna pulled an ampoule of vaccine from a box, turned it upside down, and jabbed the syringe needle in the end.

"How are the vaccine stocks holding out?" she asked.

"Fine. I just hope all the parents bring their kids to

get a shot."

"Of course they will when they know it's Dr. Mac doing the asking." Her lips quirked mischievously before she turned her attention to the next patient.

"Hey there, sweetheart." Lorna smiled at the little girl standing in front of her, fingers in her mouth as she hung on to her mother's skirts. "We just need to give you a little prick in your arm."

Lorna supported the child's arm, swabbed the skin, and administered the shot. The child watched with huge, dark eyes that tugged at Blair's heart. At least this little one was not malnourished.

The mother and child moved away, leaving space for another mother and child to step up. Lorna repeated her task, a kind smile, a few reassuring words, and another jab. She was the one with the magic touch, not him. Children loved her—even when she was poking needles in their arms. It was a shame she didn't have kids of her own. Although the mere thought of her having another man's baby tormented Blair.

He wanted her to be happy, but part of him would die if she fell in love with someone else. He'd made do with being *only* her friend because there was nobody special in her life.

As Blair turned to answer the call of another nurse, the rattle of gunfire sounded not far away.

His heart lurched, and sweat prickled down his back. Tension thrummed through the hospital tent. Women grabbed their children close, their faces all turning towards the noise in startled awareness. Gunfire in the camp meant only one thing.

"Rebels," Lorna said, voicing everyone's fears.

Blair met the soft gray of her gaze, fearing she was right but not wanting to agree until he was sure. He squeezed her shoulder. "Just sit tight for the moment."

He strode through the crowd, the people parting to let him pass. At the hospital entrance, he stepped into the alleyway. Shielding his eyes with a hand, he squinted against the bright sunlight. Male voices shouted, then someone screamed and more gunfire rent the air. The metallic rattle chilled his blood.

In the distance, figures scattered. The line of women and children waiting for vaccinations broke up, but they were at risk out in the open. "Come this way." Blair waved his arm, indicating they should enter the hospital tent. The rebel soldiers didn't respect much, but maybe the red cross on the canvas would lend these women and children some protection.

Those who'd been waiting patiently in line all charged inside the tent, pressing towards the back. They crouched with their children huddled to their sides.

Lorna hurried to him, a frown creasing her forehead. "What's going on?"

"Not sure yet, but these people are safer out of sight."

More gunfire. His gaze once again sought Lorna's. She bit her lip, her eyes shimmering with fear. Sitting together in the darkness under a canopy of a trillion stars, they sometimes talked about what would happen if rebel soldiers attacked the refugee camp. He and Lorna both knew that as Westerners, they were seriously at risk if that happened.

They'd be safer working within the boundary of Rejerrah city, where NATO forces would protect them. But the children who needed their help were out here.

As Blair stared into Lorna's wide eyes, a frisson of feeling passed between them like a whispered promise. He would protect her from harm or die trying. Military medics did *not* request a posting to Africa unless they were masochists. But Blair had volunteered. Lorna worked here with the medical charity, and he needed to be on hand in case she needed him.

"Down," Blair said to the few women still standing,

motioning with his hand so they understood. They crouched, pulling their children into their arms, shushing those who cried. The nurses moved around, softly answering questions, and soothing the most fearful.

Blair went back to the tent entrance and unfastened the cord holding one of the flaps open. Lorna did the same on the other side of the doorway. The canvas sheets slapped closed, robbing them of any breeze.

Sweat beaded on Blair's skin, and prickled his scalp. He peered through the gap in the canvas, watching the alley.

"Blair," Lorna whispered. "You need to hide. If rebel soldiers see your uniform, they'll shoot you."

The frantic look in her eyes made him squeeze her hand in reassurance, but she was right. If the rebel soldiers glimpsed a British Army uniform, they would shoot first and ask questions later. Being an unarmed doctor would not protect him. All he could do was pray they didn't come this way.

Another volley of gunfire rent the air, followed by screaming—much closer now.

"Blair, please hide." Lorna gripped his hand in both of hers.

"I'm not going to cower at the back of the hospital tent behind the women and children."

That might be the sensible thing to do, but as a British army officer, a doctor, and a proud Scotsman, such a thing was unthinkable. Instinct kept him firmly planted in front of the women and children, even if he had no weapon to protect them.

If he died, he would die with honor. His only regret would be losing Lorna. Not that she had ever been his anyway. Her heart had always belonged to his brother.

"Go and look after the children, Lorna. Please."

Tears glistened in her eyes as she nodded. She moved close to press a kiss to his cheek, then backed away. Wading into the frightened throng, she kneeled, and cuddled some of the children.

Blair turned his attention back to the narrow street. Five rebel soldiers came into view, firing apparently indiscriminately at the tents and shacks. They seemed intent on keeping people out of their way so they could move quickly. The sound of gunfire carried in the still, hot countryside and had probably alerted the NATO forces to trouble. Why were these rebel soldiers putting themselves at risk of capture?

Blair stepped back out of sight and prayed the rebels walked on past. Holding his breath, he listened to their voices, trying to work out what they were saying. He knew enough of their language to communicate with his patients, but these men talked too fast, the words running into each other.

Shock pulsed through him as a gun barrel poked between the tent flaps. A murmur of distress passed among the women behind him.

"Blair!" Lorna's voice was a strangled sob of distress. But he couldn't respond, couldn't drag his gaze from the entrance. The tent flaps billowed inwards as the soldiers pushed inside, guns leveled at his chest.

Blair raised his hands, his heart pounding, tensed, ready for the shots that would end his life.

"Are you Dr. Mac?" the first soldier demanded.

They knew his name? Blair hesitated before he answered. "Yes."

The man jerked his gun barrel at Blair. One of the other soldiers stepped up and prodded him in the back with his weapon, urging him forward.

Now the immediate danger of death had receded, Blair could think more clearly. "What do you want?"

"Are there other doctors here?" the rebel soldier asked.

"No. Only me. I'm the only one." They obviously needed medical help. Blair did not want them taking any of the nurses, especially Lorna. He risked a glance over his shoulder. She cowered with the children, a look of horror etched on her delicate features.

The rebel soldiers wandered farther into the tent. The women scrambled aside, clutching their children as guns waved over their heads.

"You doctor?" they demanded of each Western nurse. The women recoiled, shaking their heads.

The leader of the rebels pointed at the tables laden with medical supplies at the back of the hospital tent, and barked a command to his men.

One of the soldiers pulled Lorna to her feet and shoved her towards the supplies.

Blair's heart nearly beat out of his chest. "No. She's not a doctor." He tried to step towards her and earned a jab in the belly with a gun.

Fists clenched helplessly at his sides, he watched in silence as a soldier pointed a weapon at Lorna while she grabbed handfuls of dressings, medical implements, and pharmaceuticals, and shoved them into the bags that had been used to transport the vaccine.

Standing there with a gun pressed into his side and sweat pouring down his back, he prayed, pleading with God to make them leave Lorna here.

"Enough," the rebel leader shouted. Some of the soldiers grabbed the bags Lorna had filled, another held her arm and dragged her along. She stumbled, trying not to step on anyone as the man pushed her towards Blair.

They shoved the bags at Blair and Lorna to carry, then the group rushed out of the tent and set off at a trot, their guttural curses urging Blair to run faster. He angled his head, searching the sky for a NATO helicopter. Their only hope was if help arrived now. Once the rebels took them out of the refugee camp, they would disappear into the rough, hilly landscape to the north. Any chance of rescue after that was slim to none.

Chapter Two

Lorna ran along the dusty alley between the huts. The bag of medical supplies hanging from her shoulder bumped awkwardly against her leg. Her heart thundered in her ears, her breath coming in ragged gasps.

Rational thought deserted her. A fuzzy sense of shock and unreality swamped her senses. This couldn't be happening. Not to her. She'd worked in the refugee camp near Rejerrah for four years, and the rebels had never entered the camp.

She'd developed a false sense of security surrounded by these people who needed her help and welcomed her presence. But where were they now?

An unnatural silence hung over the camp, the streets empty, not a soul to be seen.

She slowed to transfer the bag to her other shoulder and earned a sharp rebuke from the soldier at her back. He pushed her, making her stagger forward. She might have fallen if Blair hadn't caught her, and supported her until she found her feet.

Blair...her best friend; her rock in troubled times. No matter what happened, he was always there for her.

She tripped in a pothole. He gripped her hand, steadying her even though he was loaded with two bags of heavy medical equipment. She glanced his way, met the blue of his gaze, calm and reassuring.

They turned a corner to see a stationary military

truck up ahead. Two rebel soldiers stood guard. As they approached, the men jumped in the cab and the engine roared to life.

The soldiers behind them shouted instructions that she couldn't understand, pushing her towards the back of the vehicle. Lorna tossed the bag she was carrying inside to join the two Blair had thrown in. He jumped onto the bed of the truck and offered his hand. She scrambled up.

Before they could sit down, the vehicle lurched off. They staggered into each other, dropped to the dusty metal floor, and were thrown around as the truck jolted over the rough ground. Two of the soldiers hung off the back, firing behind them as they made their escape.

"Look." Blair gripped her arm and pointed.

Far in the distance, little more than a dot in the sky, a helicopter was coming from the airfield at Rejerrah where the NATO forces were based. Her heart flew for a moment, buoyed by the promise of rescue before she realized it was so far away it would never reach them in time.

The vehicle swerved between the hillocks of rough ground, and she concentrated on bracing herself so she wasn't bounced around like a pea on a drum.

Blair hooked a hand over the tailgate. "Hold on to me."

She did, clinging to him for dear life, wishing she could bury her face in the front of his shirt and give way to tears. But that was out of the question. She wouldn't burden him with extra worry.

"I can't see the helicopter anymore. Not sure if it was an Apache or a Lynx."

One of their captors shouted at them to get back. He kicked the top of the tailgate, barely missing Blair's fingers as he whipped them out of the way.

They skidded across the bed of the vehicle, ending in a heap at the far side among the bags of medical supplies. Grit tore at Lorna's clothes and grazed her elbows. Blair swore under his breath and gathered her into his arms, pulling her on top of him so his body cushioned hers from the worst of the bumps.

The engine roared as the vehicle struggled up an incline, and they slid across the floor again. Lorna put her lips to his ear. "Doesn't having me on top make you more uncomfortable?"

She stared into his eyes, so close she could see every one of his thick, dark lashes, such a contrast to the bright blue of his eyes.

He laughed softly. "Sweetheart, you have no idea."

Before she could fathom what he meant, the vehicle swung around a sharp bend and sent them careening towards the front of the truck. Blair's head banged the bulkhead with a thump that must have hurt.

He closed his eyes for a moment but said nothing. They pulled themselves up to a sitting position, bracing their feet and hands to stabilize as best they could for the rest of the journey. By the time the vehicle stopped and the soldiers shouted for them to get out, Lorna was battered, bruised, and exhausted from the ride.

They jumped out into the hellish landscape to the north of Rejerrah. Like the surface of an alien planet, heaps of sand covered in sharp rocks stretched out in all directions, making it almost impassable for vehicles. NATO frequently sent foot patrols across this area, searching for the rebel base.

The men threw camouflage netting over the vehicle and led off, shouting at Lorna and Blair to follow. Each lugging a bag of medical equipment, they scrambled up a stony incline on all fours and slipped and skidded down the other side. Lorna's sneakers provided poor protection on this ground. Soon her feet were bruised and her hands grazed.

The bag weighed Lorna down until her legs ached, while pain beat relentlessly behind her eyes from the punishing sun. Sweat soaked her T-shirt and trickled down her spine. She'd heard NATO troops complain that this area north of Rejerrah where the rebels hid out was like hell on earth. They had not exaggerated.

At the sound of a helicopter approaching, Lorna's spirits leaped, but the soldiers shoved her and Blair down between the rocks and lay over them, hiding them from view beneath the camouflage of their scruffy uniforms.

The man who pressed her down against the stony ground stank of stale sweat. She gagged, her mouth so dry her tongue felt swollen. For a moment she wondered if she could go on. With legs like rubber, every square inch of her body ached. Her energy had leached away into the hot desert air.

Just when she thought she couldn't walk another pace, Blair was there beside her, his strong hand beneath her arm, pulling her up. "We must keep going. If they think you can't make it, they might shoot you."

"I need a drink," she mumbled.

"Water," Blair demanded in the native language.

One of the soldiers uncapped a canteen and passed it across. Lorna sipped, her strength and determination refreshed by the tepid liquid. Blair took a quick drink and handed it back to the soldier.

"Come on, quickly." The leader of the group seemed to be the only one who spoke English. He had taken a moment to light a cigarette as they drank. He put it between his lips and slogged on up the hill. Lorna followed, Blair right behind her, catching her arm and urging her on when she flagged.

A short while later, they scrambled down a stony gully, and followed the leader through a narrow gap into a cave. He switched on a flashlight, picking out a tunnel before them. They descended under the ground until the temperature grew more bearable. The tunnel opened into a huge cavern.

Lit by lanterns placed at intervals on the rocks, about fifty soldiers moved around, talking, cleaning weapons, and preparing food.

"No wonder the air reconnaissance can't find this base," Blair whispered.

"Come," the leader said to them. They followed him along a well-trodden path between the boulders. Hostile stares branded them as they passed, but there was something else in the faces of these men as they glared at Lorna, something predatory that made every hair on her body stand on end.

Blair must have noticed too. His arm came around her, protectively pulling her close as the rebel soldiers all stopped what they were doing to watch them.

At the side of the cavern, they entered a small chamber. The stink of blood and sickness filled the stale air. Along one side of the room, injured men lay on the ground, six casualties in all.

This must be their field hospital, but no one was tending the sick.

"Do you have a medic?" Blair asked the rebel leader, voicing Lorna's thoughts.

The man pointed at one of the casualties. "Our women say you heal with the touch of your hand, Dr. Mac. You will touch our doctor first."

Blair could hardly believe they'd been brought here because of his crazy reputation as a magical healer. It was his fault they'd been kidnapped. His gaze flashed to Lorna to gauge her reaction.

"I treated the Dr. Mac cult as a silly joke," she whispered incredulously.

She obviously didn't hold him responsible. And the reason they'd been kidnapped was academic now. They just had to deal with it.

Tension raced up Blair's spine as he glanced over the six men on the ground. Three were groaning in pain and obviously conscious. As for the other three...

Blair dragged a hand over his face and steeled himself. He'd done the usual rotation in the emergency room during his training. But he was no trauma surgeon. At least being stationed in Africa meant he'd seen and heard far more about emergency surgery than pediatricians normally did.

He glanced at Lorna's troubled expression and tried to smile with encouragement, but as he stretched his lips, it felt more like a grimace.

He kneeled beside the rebel doctor and Lorna crouched at his side. Someone had stripped the man's upper body and wrapped a tight bandage around his ribs. The intention was good, but if the ribs were broken it was the wrong thing to do. The patient would be at increased risk of pneumonia because he couldn't breathe deeply. Blair pressed his lips together and drew in a calming breath.

"Gloves, please," he said to Lorna. She pulled a pack out of the supply bag and handed them over.

Tapping the injured doctor on the shoulder, Blair tried to rouse him. "Can you hear me?"

The man moaned and opened his eyes. His gaze widened at the sight of Blair's uniform.

"Do you understand English?" Blair asked.

"Yes, I've worked in London." The man's voice was stilted with pain, but it was clear this man spoke English with a French accent.

Blair frowned. The doctor didn't sound like a native. Come to think of it, beneath the blast damage that marred his skin, he didn't look like one either. "How did you come to be working for them?" Blair tipped his head to indicate the soldier behind him, and the man on the ground obviously took his meaning.

"They captured me from the government hospital in Rejerrah. I'm SSA."

So this was no rebel doctor. He was one of the

French military medics who'd been working with the government forces. Blair rubbed his face on his sleeve. The stakes had just gone up. "I'm Major Blair Mackenzie of the British Army. I'll do my best for you."

"You're a surgeon?" the man asked.

With a wince, Blair shook his head. "A pediatrician."

The man's eyelids fell and his breath rushed out in obvious disappointment.

Blair checked the injured doctor's pulse and examined him. Multiple lacerations and contusions from the blast made his condition look worse than it was. A few of the wounds needed stitching, but none were serious. The only troublesome injury was the ribs. Broken ribs were always painful, and the man might have bleeding into the chest wall.

On cursory examination, he appeared to be the least seriously wounded of the six casualties. Yet the supplies they'd brought from the hospital would barely be sufficient to treat him.

Blair tapped the man's shoulder again. "What's your name?"

His eyes flickered open. "Remy."

"Do you have a medical kit, Remy?"

"Yes. Not much but..." The man winced and gasped in a breath, obviously in pain.

Blair glanced over his shoulder at the rebel who'd brought them here. "Where are the medical supplies this doctor used to treat his patients?"

The soldier had been smoking. The acrid smell of his cigarette further poisoned the already stale air. The man dropped the butt, stamped on it, and turned to shout over his shoulder. A few moments later, two soldiers came in lugging a crate between them. The lid was twisted and hanging off, while blast marks peppered the metal sides. They set it down close by.

"This is all we have."

Blair and Lorna rose and crouched beside the

16

container, sorting through what was held inside. The box had probably been in the same explosion as the doctor, but some of the contents had survived. There were a couple of unit one packs that would normally be carried by a combat medic—obviously stolen from the government forces.

With a sigh of relief, Blair noted IV fluids and tubing, supplies for the control of blood loss and for airway management, along with morphine, antibiotics, and other medicines.

He had what he needed to treat the French doctor, but the man really needed to be transferred to a properly equipped field hospital for a thorough examination in case he had internal injuries.

While Lorna set up a drip to administer fluids and antibiotics to Remy and took his temperature, Blair went along the line of patients and did an initial assessment of each. All were alive, but two were unconscious. He did his best to help them, administering pain relief and antibiotics.

"Do you have water for washing?" he asked the guard.

"No. Only for drinking."

"Can we have a drink?" Lorna asked.

The soldier shook his head. "You cure our doctor first."

Cure! Blair hung his head and stared at the ground, the hopelessness of the situation getting to him. Should he tell the guard that the doctor needed a hospital?

Lorna touched his arm and met his gaze. His feelings of defeat were reflected in her eyes. There was little they could do for most of these men. When the rebels realized that, they would have no further use for him or Lorna.

He couldn't let that happen. He had to protect her.

Sucking in a fortifying breath, Blair turned his attention back to Remy. This poor French doctor needed treatment. Blair would do his best to help him. He moved a lantern to the rocky shelf above the patient while Lorna laid out a paper wrapper and placed on it the lidocaine, syringe, suture materials, and dressings.

Blair pulled on a clean pair of nitrile gloves, then removed the binding from the doctor's ribs, and proceeded to clean and stitch his wounds. At least if the NATO forces found them, Remy would stand a good chance of recovery.

After Blair and Lorna had tended all six men, they flopped on the ground on the opposite side of the cave from the patients. Blair had no idea what the time was or how long they'd been working. He checked his phone to discover it was late evening, but there was no signal underground. He did snap a few photos of the cave and the casualties.

He and Lorna consumed the water and food they'd been given, and tried to get comfortable.

"There's no guard," Lorna whispered. The soldier who spoke English had watched them for a while, then disappeared after he'd given them something to eat and drink.

"They don't need anyone to watch us. Every man in that cavern out there is a guard. We can't escape without going through it."

Lorna heaved a resigned sigh and lay down.

"Come here. Rest your head on me." Blair extended an arm to make her a pillow.

She glanced at him, blinking sleepily. A burst of emotion filled him, hope tinged with fear. He rolled on his side and pulled her close. Ignoring the discomfort of the hard ground, he shut out everything except the feel of her body in his arms, and the smell of her hair.

He loved this woman so much it hurt. Every day he wanted to tell her, yet every day he rejected the idea. Ten years ago he'd said those three little words and it nearly wrecked their friendship. After that he'd kept his feelings to himself, frightened he might lose her completely.

But if this was the end of the line, maybe the time had come to let her know that she was the only woman he'd ever loved, and he would love her until the moment he died.

Chapter Three

Lorna curled up against Blair, her head on his chest, the steady beat of his heart beneath her ear. She was exhausted but she couldn't sleep. The thought she might not have long on this earth concentrated her mind on how she'd lived her life and what was important.

A terrible sense of remorse assailed her. All her adult life Blair had been there for her when she needed him, but she'd always held part of herself back from him.

At first it was because she'd been angry with his family. If Sir Robert Mackenzie didn't think she was good enough for his precious son Duncan, she wanted nothing to do with any of the Mackenzies.

Yet Blair wouldn't take the hint. No matter how many times she didn't return his calls, he'd still kept trying. He was loyal and had never let her down. Not once. Yet holding a little of herself back had become a habit.

She'd been crazy to behave this way. Blair deserved to be judged by his own actions, not those of his family. He'd accepted her on her own merits, yet she'd done exactly what she'd blamed Sir Robert of doing to her, and judged Blair on his social status and family name.

It didn't matter if his father owned a castle and her

mother had cleaned for them and washed their clothes. Blair might have noble Scottish blood running through his veins but he was just a man, a good man, and she was a coward for not facing up to the demons that kept them apart.

"Blair," she whispered. "Are you asleep?"

"No."

In all the years they'd known each other, they'd never discussed the reason why Sir Robert Mackenzie had stopped her dating Duncan. It had been a taboo subject. Even now she couldn't bring herself to confide her fear that her mother had something to do with the falling out. It was easier to put all the blame on his father.

"Your father thinks I'm not good enough for your family. He thinks I'm a nobody." The hurtful words Sir Robert had said were branded on her brain. She could still hear his furious tone when he accused her of being a grasping little nobody with her claws in Duncan.

"You're not a *nobody*, Lorna." Blair raised his head and propped it on his hand. He caressed her hair, gently stroking wisps behind her ear. "You're the most important *somebody* in the world to me."

Tears filled Lorna's eyes. She buried her face against his chest, breathing in the scent of him. He smelled of the dust and heat of Africa, along with something unique that reminded her of the cool Caledonia pine forests and misty mountains of Scotland.

He was her man. There had never been anyone else. All these years he'd been *the one* and she'd never acknowledged it because Blair was a link to a past she wanted to forget.

His hand stroked soothing circles on her back, and his lips pressed the top of her head, his breath warm against her hair.

"I still love you, Lorna."

A lump clogged her throat. God help her, she'd

known it for so long and let him love her without offering anything in return. When Duncan showed an interest in her, she'd been flattered, and her mother had pushed her to "catch herself a laird." But all along it had been Blair she had feelings for. Why did she wait until they were in danger before being honest?

"I love you too, Blair."

He hugged her close, holding her so tightly she could barely breathe. "Why did you never tell me?"

"Why didn't you tell me?" she retorted, not wanting to dig into all the reasons she'd held back.

He laughed sadly. "I did, my love. I did."

Lorna squeezed her eyes closed, remembering that night, the dinner, the red roses, the diamond ring. A few months after Duncan dropped her like the proverbial hot potato, Blair turned twenty. He said it didn't matter that she was older than him now they were both in their twenties and proposed out of the blue.

She'd been so angry and confused after the argument with her mother and what Sir Robert said to her, she'd lashed out at Blair.

"I said some horrible things that night. I'm really sorry. It was aimed at Duncan and your father." And my mother.

"I know, love."

Lorna lifted her head and wiped her teary eyes with the side of her hand. She stared into the handsome face of this amazing man. He was the love of her life, and she had never even kissed him.

"How did you get to be so wise and understanding, Blair Mackenzie?"

"I'm not. I'm just a man in love."

The solitary lantern cast two small dancing flames in his eyes. On the hard cave floor, in the hellish land north of Rejerrah, she pressed her lips to those of the man she loved and vowed never to let him down again.

***

Lorna woke, curled on her side on the hard ground. The blissful unconsciousness of sleep fled quickly. She sat up, noticing the pad of dressings that Blair must have placed under her head as a pillow.

The memory of lying in his arms and the kisses they'd shared filled her with warmth and happiness even in this dark place. How she regretted all those wasted years when they could have been a couple, but such feelings would achieve nothing. She must be positive and make the most of the time they had left together.

A solitary lantern still lit the cave, making it impossible to judge if it were day or night. She pulled out her phone to check the time, but the battery was dead.

A short distance away, Blair sat on the ground beside Remy's makeshift bed. They talked softly about their experiences with the rebels. As Lorna rose, she caught Blair's eye.

"Good morning. How did you sleep?" he asked.

"Okay, surprisingly." She must have been totally exhausted, because she hadn't roused even though she'd had to bed down on the hard ground. "How about you?"

"The sound sleep of a happy man."

He smiled as he pushed to his feet and approached. He wrapped his arms around her, bending his head to press a kiss to her lips. Where his fingers brushed her skin, she tingled, and his kiss brought a sigh of longing to her lips.

Lorna lowered her eyes, suddenly shy. In all the years they'd been friends, she'd never felt like this before. Her nerves hummed with possibilities, a subtle tension between them like electricity sparking in the air. It was as if a switch had been flipped inside her. All the feelings she'd denied for so long had been released

23

to run riot through her body.

Blair took her hand and led her towards the Frenchman. "Remy's told me about the other rebel camps and described where they are. If we get out of this alive, that will help the NATO patrols."

"Good morning, Lorna," Remy said. "Thank you for helping me yesterday."

"We're going to try operating on a couple of the men," Blair said. "Remy's a trauma specialist."

"I can only watch and advise," Remy added. "It hurts to breathe, so I can't use my hands yet."

"How were you injured?" Lorna asked.

Remy rolled his eyes. "We were on our way here to pick up two wounded men. The foolish driver ran over one of their own IEDs."

Lorna laughed. It wasn't really funny—men had been hurt. But honestly, the irony...

After a quick drink of water, Lorna and Blair prepped to operate. It was impossible to achieve anything near sterile conditions, but they were trained to help people and they planned to do their best.

They each grasped one of Remy's upper arms and slowly raised him to a sitting position. He closed his eyes, his breath shallow and pained. "I've always told my patients that broken ribs hurt a lot. I didn't know how much until now."

After he'd steeled himself for more discomfort, he nodded and they helped him to his feet. He leaned heavily on Blair for a good five minutes. Finally he opened his eyes and walked gingerly to and fro. "Okay, let's get started."

Blair had identified the two men most likely to benefit from surgery. Blair and Lorna scrubbed up as best they could with alcohol wipes before donning nitrile gloves and paper gowns. With Remy narrating the procedure, Lorna kneeled at Blair's side and followed the instructions she was given.

By what would have been lunchtime, they were done. She rose from the second patient, her knees aching from the hard ground. Stretching out her tense back, she stripped off her gloves and gown.

Although they could hear the sound of the rebel soldiers talking in the cavern, they hadn't seen a guard since they woke. Lorna was happy to keep it that way. The rebel soldiers unsettled her.

The English-speaking guard finally put in an appearance with some army ration packs and another bottle of water. He paused inside the cave entrance and gaped at Remy, where he stood beside Blair. His startled gaze moved from the Frenchman to Blair, then back.

"You cured our doctor."

"He needs rest for his ribs to heal," Blair insisted in his professional voice.

The soldier came farther into the cave, his gun slung over his shoulder, and placed the food and water on the ground. He circled Remy as if he couldn't believe his eyes.

"The women said you had the touch of a shaman, Dr. Mac. It's true."

Blair's lips flattened in a look of irritation. Lorna placed a calming hand on his back. His crazy mystical reputation annoyed him, but now was not the time to deny it. If the rebels thought Blair really did wield a healing force, they might treat him better.

The soldier backed away, his expression thoughtful as he left the cave.

She and Blair helped Remy lie down again, then sat close to him and tore open the ration packs. As they ate, angry voices came from the main cavern.

Remy stilled and listened. "They're arguing about you, Blair," he said. "Kibwe, the English-speaking guard, wants to take you to the village where his family lives so you can treat his son."

"The others don't agree?" Lorna asked.

"Kibwe's a captain, and an educated man. He was a teacher before the war. Hence his grasp of English. He usually gets his way."

As Lorna ripped open a cereal bar and took a bite, Kibwe returned to their cave, his gun still slung over his shoulder. Another soldier trailed behind him, scowling.

"You will come with me, Dr. Mac," Kibwe said.

Blair's gaze flicked to Lorna, a flash of hope in his eyes. Excited tension raced along her limbs, firing up her flagging energy. The chance of escape was much better if they were outside. Blair vaulted to his feet and extended a hand to help Lorna up.

"No, only Dr. Mac." Kibwe shook his head and gestured for Lorna to sit down again. Lorna's heart pounded, sweat prickling her skin as panic surged through her. If Blair left her alone with the soldiers, she'd be terrified.

"I won't leave her." Blair's tone brooked no argument.

Kibwe pulled the gun off his shoulder and waved it in the air.

"You will come alone, Dr. Mac."

Blair shook his head, his feet rooted to the spot.

The African narrowed his eyes at Blair, then blew out a breath and nodded. "All right. The nurse can come, but hurry up. I want to get out of here."

Lorna crouched at Remy's side. She felt guilty about leaving him behind. He was as much a captive as they were. "You'll be okay?"

"Go," he said. "I'll heal."

"Bring a bag of medical supplies," Kibwe ordered.

Blair grabbed one of the bags and added a few of the items from the unit one packs before fastening the straps and hoisting it over his shoulder.

Lorna tensed as they stepped into the main cavern, dreading the march through the glowering rebel troops, but the space was nearly deserted. "Where is everyone?" she whispered to Blair.

"Must be on a mission."

Kibwe was visibly agitated and kept urging them to hurry. It seemed like he wanted them out of there before the others returned. Lorna was happy to comply. She and Blair trotted to keep pace with the two soldiers, eager to be away.

They emerged from the tunnel into the heat of the afternoon sun. It blinded Lorna for a moment, but the two Africans seemed unaffected. They yanked a camouflage net off a jeep and gestured for Lorna and Blair to climb in the back.

The two soldiers sat up front, Kibwe driving, the other one with his gun resting on his lap.

If she and Blair were ever going to escape, this was their chance. But that would still leave them out in the middle of nowhere, with no water.

Blair squeezed Lorna's hand to attract her attention and raised his eyebrows. "Follow my lead," he mouthed silently.

She nodded. Blair obviously had an escape plan. Lorna wasn't sure how they could get back to Rejerrah on foot. If the rebels didn't catch up with them, the sun would probably finish them off.

Chapter Four

Blair decided that whatever happened, he and Lorna must make sure they were not taken back inside the rebels' underground camp. NATO patrols had been searching for that camp for months. The chance of rescue from there was one in a million.

No. The best chance of escape was to make a dash for it while they were being moved. There were only two guards with them, and one was driving. Blair was not combat trained, but he'd been shooting on his home estate in Scotland since he was strong enough to hold a rifle steady, and the army trained all doctors to handle a gun for their own protection.

The jeep jolted over the rough ground, bouncing them around. Blair braced his legs, grasped the door, and gripped the seat behind Lorna so she could lean into him for support. This country must be hell on a vehicle's suspension. And he'd thought the Scottish lanes were rough.

"How far are we going?" he asked Kibwe. He wanted an idea of how long they had to make their escape.

"You'll see," the man shouted over his shoulder. Blair obviously wasn't going to get any more out of him.

It was best to try to make their move on the outward journey. On the way back, there might be more guards. The position of the sun indicated they were heading east. That meant they would be parallel with Rejerrah and possibly closer to it than they had been at the camp. To reach civilization, they would have to walk due south.

The jeep bumped over a rock, bouncing Lorna so high she nearly fell out of the jeep. Blair caught hold of her and pulled her close, wrapping his arm around her shoulders.

Even in the midst of this terrible situation, the pleasure of holding her and knowing she loved him eased a tension inside that he'd lived with forever. Her love meant so much it was like a fire spurring him on to freedom, spurring him on to live when hope seemed all but gone. He wanted his future with Lorna; he wanted his own children. He wanted what his sister, Megan, had with Daniel, and what Duncan had with Naomi.

For so long he'd thought he was destined to walk through life alone. Now he had everything to live for. He would not give up his happy future without a fight.

Eyes fixed on the guards to make sure they weren't watching, he pressed his lips to Lorna's ear. "If the vehicle stops, be ready to run."

She gazed at him, doubt clear on her face, but she nodded.

Before they took off, Blair must knock out at least one of the guards. If he could disable both it would be better. He clenched his fist in his lap and imagined swinging a punch at the man in front of him. That was unlikely to do the trick. He needed a weapon.

Blair hated the thought of hurting anyone; it went against everything he believed in. As a doctor, he wanted to heal people. The army had proved to be a way for him to practice his medicine in far-flung parts of the world where the people needed his help, yet he was not a military man—he was a doctor. If he lived through this, maybe he should resign from the army and join the medical charity Lorna worked for.

The vehicle engine droned as it struggled up an incline, weaving in between boulders. Kibwe was crazy to try to drive in this terrain. The other rebel soldier obviously agreed as he started to complain.

Their two guards snapped angry words at each other, their attention distracted. Blair dangled a hand over the side of the jeep and snagged a loose chip of rock. Now he had his weapon. In a few more seconds, when the jeep reached the top of the hill, he'd strike.

As he adjusted his grip on the rock, a truck engine revved behind them. Blair and Lorna both swiveled in their seats to glance back. A rebel truck with men hanging off the sides came into view over a hill.

Blair cursed under his breath. Had they missed their chance to escape? Kibwe looked back and noticed the truck. He floored the gas and the jeep crested the hill and roared down the other side, bouncing around like a rowboat in a storm.

Blair forgot all thoughts of escape and concentrated on hanging on to Lorna and keeping his seat. The jeep lurched drunkenly, clipping the boulders. Knocked off course, it careened forward and smashed into a rock, nearly tossing them into the front.

Gunfire sounded behind them.

"Are they shooting at us?" Lorna shouted over the roar of the jeep's engine as Kibwe tried to back up, the tires throwing up a choking cloud of dust.

"Sounds like it," Blair shouted.

Far from escaping, they were about to be mown down in the crossfire between warring factions of rebels.

Another sound joined the chaos, a far more welcome one. The drone of a helicopter engine grew rapidly as the huge bulk of a NATO Lynx helicopter bore down on the jeep.

Blair waved his arms, a smile of relief on his face despite the desperate plight they were in. All hell was about to break loose and he needed to get Lorna out of the jeep and behind cover. The two guards jumped out, shouting at Blair and Lorna to come with them.

Blair vaulted over the vehicle's door, lifted Lorna out, then gripped her hand. They sprinted away towards the nearest large rocks. At that moment, the rebel truck appeared over the hill directly behind them. Gunfire rattled, peppering the ground all around. In answer, the door-mounted machine gun on the Lynx discharged, throwing up a trail of dirt and splintering rocks.

As they ran towards the rocks, Blair put himself between Lorna and the rebels. They had nearly reached safety when something punched him in the lower back. He stumbled, his legs suddenly weak. He went down on his knees. For a moment he was confused. Had he been hit? It didn't hurt.

He pressed a hand to his back, feeling the wet fabric of his shirt. His hand came away red. As he stared at the blood, his brain refused to process.

"Blair." Lorna screamed his name, grabbed the front of his shirt, and dragged him behind the rocks. He flopped onto his back and gazed up at her. An aura of darkness ringed his vision, a cool, welcoming darkness that promised peace.

The last thing he heard was Lorna's voice calling his name.

Lorna frantically pulled open Blair's shirt to reveal a bullet exit wound on his abdomen. At the sight of the damage, the blood drained from her head, leaving her ears humming. She'd seen all sorts of injuries during her nursing career, but it was very different when someone you loved was hurt.

"Blair, stay with me." She cupped her hand around his face. Two days' growth of stubble prickled her palm. His eyelashes stayed closed against his tanned cheeks.

He wasn't responding.

For a panicked moment she felt for his pulse. As she found it, she noticed his chest rising and falling. Tears of relief filled her eyes, but she dashed them away. He might be alive, but he needed immediate medical care.

The NATO helicopter landed a hundred yards away. British troops jumped out and advanced, exchanging fire with the rebels who'd arrived in the truck. An Apache battlefield attack helicopter angled down out of the sky and fired on the rebels, forcing them to take cover.

Lorna stood and gazed towards the British soldiers. She waved her arms and shouted to attract their attention. "Help. Man down."

A soldier with a medical pack on his back ran over and dropped to his knees at Blair's side. "Major Mackenzie, can you hear me, sir?"

The medic pulled off his pack and staunched the flow of blood from Blair's wounds, covering them with field dressings. He took Blair's vitals, then stood and signaled to bring over the stretcher.

"Are you all right, Ms. Bell," he asked.

She nodded. "Just look after Blair."

Two soldiers lifted Blair onto the stretcher, strapped him securely, and ran back to the helicopter.

Lorna ran with them, her gaze hardly leaving Blair's still, pale face. The thought of losing him swirled like ice water in her belly. Please let him live, she prayed. Now they'd escaped, they had so much to live for.

The soldiers loaded the stretcher and one of them extended a hand to help her climb in the helicopter. The medic worked on Blair, setting up a drip.

"How is he?" Lorna asked, her voice trembling with tension.

"The bullet made a clean exit. His recovery will depend on what sort of internal damage it caused passing through."

Lorna kneeled beside Blair, gripping his limp hand. She tried to be positive and reassure herself he would be all right. But her heart thumped so hard she found it difficult to draw air into her lungs.

Blair groaned and rolled his head from side to side.

"Major Mackenzie, sir, can you hear me?" The medic gripped his shoulder. "You're safe, sir. We're taking you back to the field hospital at Rejerrah."

Blair's eyes flickered open, then closed again. "Lorna," he mumbled.

"I'm here, love." She squeezed his hand.

"Rebel base underground." Blair gasped a couple of pained breaths before he continued. "Three klicks west."

"Oh, and there's a French doctor being held captive underground, so be careful," Lorna added, remembering Remy.

The medic shouted the information to the pilot and the message was passed on. A radio crackled and beeped as they reported their position and took orders.

"We're to take Major Mackenzie back to base, then head out here again," the medic said. "Hang on."

The helicopter engine droned as the aircraft lifted off, the din so loud there was no point trying to talk. The floor vibrated beneath Lorna's bruised knees. The smell of aviation fuel and oil filled her nose.

For the first time since she'd been taken from the hospital tent, Lorna relaxed. Exhaustion swept through her, the feeling so intense she could barely keep her eyes open. Blinking wearily, she gripped Blair's hand with a gentle pressure so he knew she was with him.

The helicopter set down at the military airport on the outskirts of Rejerrah. Lorna moved aside as the medics lifted Blair from the aircraft. They ran the hundred yards to the field hospital.

Following behind them, Lorna walked as fast as her fatigued muscles allowed. As she pushed through the double doors into the medical facility, doctors and nurses in scrubs rushed along the corridor. Blair was carried into a room, then the army medic who'd delivered him dashed off to rejoin his unit.

Lorna kept out of the way, biting her lip as they stripped Blair's clothes and prepped him for surgery. It clenched her heart to see this strong, competent man she loved lying there helpless and in pain. She moved into his line of sight and smiled. "Love you," she mouthed, hoping he could read her lips.

The small smile on his face as his eyelids drooped told her he understood.

A pretty doctor with wavy dark hair pinned back under a scrub cap put an IV in the back of his hand. "Looks like you've earned an early Christmas holiday, Mackenzie. You've had us all worried, you know."

Blair's eyes flickered open again and the woman smiled down at him. "Hold tight, my darling. We'll have you on a plane back to bonnie Scotland soon."

They moved him to a gurney and wheeled him towards the OR.

"Lorna," Blair said, angling his head to search for her.

"I'm here." She stepped up to the gurney and walked beside it as they travelled the corridor.

"You okay?" Blair croaked, his face creased with pain.

"Don't worry about me." Lorna brushed her fingertips across his cheek, then someone held aside the plastic strip curtains to the OR and Blair disappeared inside.

Lorna leaned against the corridor wall, her shoulder resting on the cold cement block, listening to the medical staff talking. She could see their fuzzy outlines through the plastic curtain as they moved around Blair on the operating table.

"I'm going to put you to sleep for a little while now,

Mackenzie. Sweet dreams." The pretty anesthetist laughed as Blair mumbled something.

"You must be Lorna Bell, the charity worker who was taken hostage with Major Mackenzie." An army nurse approached along the corridor. "You look done in. You're not injured, are you?"

"No, just tired."

Lorna wanted to stand and listen to Blair's procedure, to make sure everything went well, but she was so weary she had to lean on the wall to remain upright.

"Come on. I'll find you some clean clothes and somewhere to sleep."

The nurse took her to a room that contained a bed and a plastic chair. "Here, take a seat. I'll be back in a moment."

A few minutes later, the nurse returned with a clean T-shirt and shorts, a glass of water, and some chocolate from a ration pack.

"You rest, Ms. Bell."

"Wake me when Blair comes around after the surgery."

The woman nodded as she left.

Lorna ate the chocolate, drank the water, then stripped down to her panties and put on the clean T-shirt before slipping under the bedcovers.

The next thing she knew, the nurse was touching her arm. "Blair's out of surgery and awake," she said.

Lorna blinked owlishly, feeling as though she'd only closed her eyes for a moment.

She sat up and sucked in a breath. It was dark outside, the room lit by a flickering strip light. The cooler evening temperature was a relief after being out in the sun.

After pulling on the clean shorts, she washed her face and hands in the bowl of water she'd been given, then wandered along the corridor.

Blair was sitting up in bed, sipping from a plastic cup, the pretty anesthetist on the chair beside him. The woman rose as Lorna entered and held out her hand. "Sorry, there wasn't time for introductions earlier. I'm Julia Braithwaite. Sounds as though you two had a lucky escape."

Lorna shook Julia's hand, then turned to Blair. Her gaze connected with his, her heart lifting at the familiar light back in his eyes. "You're sitting up already. How do you feel?"

"It hurts to move," he said, wincing as he braced his arms and adjusted his position.

"Mackenzie is a lucky one," Julia said. "The bullet missed all his vital organs, so he'll be raring to go again soon."

"I want to get out of bed and try walking." Blair's mouth was set in a determined line.

"Already?" Lorna's gaze shot to Julia.

"The surgeon has okayed it," she said. "With abdominal surgery, once the patient is able to take fluids by mouth, there's no reason to keep them in bed. Studies indicate that getting back on their feet aids recovery. I thought you might like to help him." Julia smiled at Lorna and she returned the expression gratefully.

"Of course. I'd love to."

"The Aeromed flight will come for him tomorrow. It'll be much better if he can go on in a wheelchair rather than on a gurney."

Lorna hadn't thought past Blair's surgery. "Can I travel with him?"

"Stop discussing me as if I'm not here." Blair's usual confident manner was back. "Of course you're coming with me." He held out a hand to Lorna and she took it, the strength of his grip such a relief. She never again wanted to see him injured and in pain.

Chapter Five

When Friedrich Nietzsche said, "That which does not kill us makes us stronger," he obviously had not endured a sponge bath given by the woman he'd loved platonically for ten years.

Blair sat on the edge of his bed in underpants. Lorna crouched in front of him with a bowl of warm water. She washed his feet then sponged down his legs, smiling sweetly and talking softly. The tortuous experience was exacerbated because it was agony every time he clenched his stomach muscles.

Once she was done with his legs, she moved on to his back. With gentle strokes of the cloth, she washed his shoulders, back, and arms. Every brush of her hand on his skin was divine torment.

Dreams of Lorna had filled Blair's sleep for so many years, he was used to controlling his reactions to her. But having her hands on his body was almost more than he could bear.

"Turn around. I'll do your chest now," she said.

"No need." Blair had to clear his throat before he could continue. "I can reach that part myself." She really had no idea what an effect she had on him. He relieved her of the cloth, turned away, and quickly did the job himself, uncaring if the water ran down and wet the dressing. He just wanted this torture over with.

A shower had been out because of the dressing, so one of the nurses came to wash him. When Lorna offered to do the job, he knew it would test him, but he couldn't turn her down without hurting her feelings. And that was the last thing he wanted to do. His family had hurt her enough.

It was a mystery to Blair why his father had come down on Lorna so hard for dating Duncan. His father was normally a reasonable man. He didn't know what his father had said, but it was enough to make her leave Scotland and never return. For a Scots lass who loved her country, that had to be something pretty awful.

"I'll just go and make us a cup of tea," Lorna said diplomatically, giving him time to finish the more personal element of the sponge bath on his own.

"Great." Blair dredged up a smile from some part of his brain that wasn't consumed with thoughts of pulling Lorna into his bed.

By the time she returned with two mugs of tea and some ration-pack snacks, Blair was back in bed and somewhat recovered.

"You didn't take your walk down the hall," she said.

"I'll do that after my tea."

She put the mugs on the small table and perched on the bed beside him. Blair took her hand, running his thumb over her palm. "Thank you, love. It feels good to be clean again."

Lorna smiled shyly and leaned in, resting her face in the curve of his neck. He wrapped his arms around her carefully, wary of his abdominal wound. It pulled, but what was a little pain in exchange for holding her.

Blair pressed his nose to her hair and breathed in the faint floral smell. Was it too soon to propose marriage? He'd been waiting so long; he wanted to make her his wife as soon as possible. But he'd rather be fit and healthy before he popped the question.

He hated being incapacitated, hated pottering up

and down the hall like a ninety-year-old, and being unable to get out there to do his job. As a doctor, he didn't enjoy being cooped up in the hospital. As a patient, it was a million times worse.

He'd never analyzed his preferences before. Now he realized his passion was for working with people in their own environment. Settling down to a traditional medical career in a hospital would never suit him. He wanted to speed up this recovery process, marry Lorna, and get back to helping the people who needed him— with her at his side.

Blair stroked Lorna's hair and kissed her temple. "You'll come back to Kindrogan with me, won't you?"

She turned uncertain gray eyes on him and bit her lip. "If your family will have me."

"Dad is hardly ever there, and Duncan will be fine about it. Don't worry. You'll like his wife and his little girl, Holly. She's very sweet. My sister and her husband have a little girl as well."

"I'd love to see Kindrogan again. I dream about it sometimes." Her wistful tone made Blair hold her tighter. The castle was as much her home as his. She'd grown up on the Kindrogan Estate in one of the estate cottages and spent her childhood there. It was wrong that his father had driven her and her mother away.

They were interrupted by a knock on the door. Lt. Col. Cameron Knight, who commanded the army Aeromed flight, put his head in. "Hope I haven't interrupted anything."

Lorna slipped off the bed, a grin on her face, Blair smiling broadly. Cameron was one of his oldest friends. They'd been at school together, and Cameron had spent many summer vacations at Kindrogan. "Good to see you."

He held out his hand and Blair shook it, then Cameron turned to Lorna, his eyebrows raised. "Lorna Bell. As pretty as ever."

"Cam, you haven't changed, you sweet-talker."

They embraced, all smiles. Blair was grateful that Cameron would remind Lorna of happy times at Kindrogan when they were children. Before life became complicated by the onset of hormones.

Cameron glanced at his watch. "Once the plane's been refueled and the equipment we shipped is unloaded, we'll be ready to head back. You're both coming, I take it?"

"Yes." Blair put an arm around Lorna's waist.

"So that's the way the wind blows, is it? Congratulations. I always thought you two would get together one day. Not sure why it took you so long."

"My fault," Lorna said softly, leaning her head against Blair's shoulder.

"Nobody's fault," Blair added firmly. He didn't want to start this relationship with guilt from the past dragging them down.

"I gather you're boarding in a wheelchair, mate," Cameron said.

Blair's spirits flopped. "So they tell me." He would much rather walk on and sit in a normal seat.

Cameron patted his shoulder. "If you saw some of the poor guys we transport back to the UK, you'd thank your lucky stars you got off so lightly."

Lorna walked beside Blair as Cameron pushed him down the ramp out of the Aeromed aircraft at RAF Brize Norton in Oxfordshire. The six-hour flight had passed quickly. Dosed up with painkillers, Blair had slept much of the way and so had Lorna.

At nearly nine p.m. in mid-December, it was dark and cold in the UK. Under the aircraft lights, frost sparkled on the blacktop while everyone's breath drifted away in smoky plumes.

"You warm enough?" Lorna rested a hand on Blair's shoulder. He was clad in pajamas, socks, a dressing gown, and covered in a couple of blankets.

"Fine. What about you?"

Beneath Lorna's shorts, goose bumps raced across the bare skin of her legs, but she was bundled up in Cameron's jacket. "I'll survive until I get inside."

An ambulance stood a short distance away, waiting to transport Blair to the military hospital. Cameron had invited Lorna to stay with his family. Blair insisted she go straight there instead of coming to the hospital with him. It was already late and they were both tired.

A limousine glided across the blacktop and came to a halt nearby. Two people climbed out and hurried towards them. Sir Robert Mackenzie strode up, his wife running in tiny steps to keep up in her high-heeled pumps.

Tall, self assured, and with an irritating air of superiority, just the sight of Sir Robert infuriated Lorna. All the things she'd dreamed of saying to him rolled through her head, the accusations and recriminations. In her daydreams she gave him a piece of her mind.

But everything had changed. Despite her suspicions about Sir Robert and her mother, if she and Blair were to have a future together, she must tread carefully. So she kept her lips pressed firmly closed.

Slim and petite, her long red hair flowing over the collar of a fur coat, Lady Mackenzie was the epitome of elegance. She rushed up to Blair and engulfed her son in a hug.

"Blair, are you all right, darling? I've been so worried. I don't want you going back to Africa. It's too dangerous."

"I'm in the army, Mum. I go where I'm posted."

"Then your father will ensure you're not posted to Africa again, won't you, Robert." She patted her husband on the arm with a pointed expression, then turned to kiss Cameron's cheek.

"Mum, Dad, you remember Lorna Bell, don't you?" Blair gripped her hand and lifted it to his lips, planting a kiss on her knuckles.

There was a moment of awkward silence while Blair's parents absorbed the message that they were a couple. Then Lady Mackenzie stepped forward a little stiffly. "Lorna, of course I remember you. How could I forget?"

Before Lorna could reply, she was swamped in a cloud of expensive perfume and fur as Blair's mother embraced her.

"I'm pleased you survived your terrible ordeal unscathed, dear. I always think that sort of thing is so much worse for a woman."

"Thank you, Lady Mackenzie. It's nice to see you again."

Sir Robert cleared his throat and passed his steely gaze over Lorna, his expression unreadable. He nodded to acknowledge her. "Ms. Bell."

"I suggest we move Blair out of the cold," Cameron said diplomatically as he beckoned the paramedics from the ambulance.

"Oh, yes." Lady Mackenzie adjusted the blankets wrapped around Blair.

"Mum, I can do that."

"Not properly, you can't. Men never tuck anything in properly."

Blair rolled his eyes, but it was plain he enjoyed the mothering. It was rather sweet, really.

Lorna snatched a quick kiss with Blair before the paramedics pushed his wheelchair onto the electric ramp at the back of the ambulance, hoisted it up, then wheeled him on board.

Since Blair came out of surgery, Lorna had been with him. She'd helped bathe him and dress him. Watching his mother climb in the back of the ambulance while she was left standing on the runway made Lorna feel strangely abandoned.

"See you tomorrow, Blair," she shouted, just before the ambulance door slammed shut.

The vehicle pulled away, its headlights cutting through the darkness. Sir Robert climbed into his limo to follow. Lorna shivered as the ambulance grew smaller and finally disappeared.

Cameron put his arm around her shoulders. "Come on. We'll go home. My wife's dying to meet you. You're quite a celebrity, you know."

"A celebrity?" Lorna had no idea what he meant.

"Yes." He led her to a large black SUV parked by the fence. He pulled out his key and popped the locks, then opened the door for her. "In the last couple of days, you and Blair have been splashed all over the media. You're big news, Ms. Bell."

He climbed in beside her and started the engine. Heat blasted and Lorna spread her cold fingers in the hot air. They accelerated across the acres of empty runway, but Cameron slowed as they approached the gate manned by army guards. The vehicle headlights illuminated a crowd of people outside.

"That's a pretty hardy bunch of reporters out here in this temperature."

"They're reporters?"

"Yep. The Ministry of Defense has released a statement, but the vultures are still hoping to get some juicy details. It's best if you don't say anything."

"Don't worry. I'd rather not talk about what happened." She wanted to put the ordeal behind her.

The guards on the gate held back the crowd, and Cameron drove through. Lorna recoiled as camera lights flashed and faces peered in the window. She felt light-headed with tiredness and a strange, surreal sense that none of this could be real.

Yet it was all too real. Blair was in the hospital, and she'd just come face-to-face with Sir Robert after ten years. Soon she would see Duncan again, and meet his wife. That would be an awkward experience.

Cameron's SUV wound through narrow country lanes. About twenty minutes later, he drove down a bumpy track. His headlights picked out a huge old farmhouse surrounded by gardens.

Christmas lights twinkled on a pine tree nearby. Lorna had been working abroad for the last five Christmases and hadn't celebrated. Being back in the UK at Christmastime would be like going back in time.

Cameron stopped the car, jumped out, and came around to open her door. Light, warmth, and the delicious smell of roast meat greeted Lorna as she walked inside the house.

A pretty woman with blonde hair and blue eyes appeared at the door at the end of the corridor, a grin on her face. "Hello, Lorna. I'm Alice. You're much prettier than the photo of you they showed on the television last night. Isn't she, Cameron?"

"Yes," Cameron said, distracted by something at the top of the stairs. "You're supposed to be in bed, young man."

A little African boy wearing Spiderman pajamas trotted downstairs, a fat Santa toy dangling from his hand. He jumped the last few steps into Cameron's arms.

After a hug and kiss, Cameron lowered the boy to the ground and crouched at his side. "Sam, this lady is called Lorna. She's going to stay with us tonight. She's been working in Africa."

The boy peered up at Lorna with a frown of curiosity. "I was born there."

"That's right." Cameron stood up, gripping his son's hand. "Lorna, this is Sami."

Lorna had heard the story of how Cameron and his wife adopted an African orphan. She could just make out the faint scar where Sami's cleft lip had been repaired, but she wouldn't have noticed the mark if she hadn't known it was there.

She smiled. "Pleased to meet you, Sami."

"I've saved you some pot roast," Alice said. "I'm sure you're tired, but come and eat before you go to bed. There are clean clothes in the spare room for you."

As Lorna followed Alice towards the kitchen, more little footsteps sounded on the stairs. She swiveled to find a cute little boy's face peering at her through the banisters.

Cameron laughed. "This is Harry. Now you've met the whole family."

"Hello, Harry."

Cameron mounted the stairs, Sami's hand in his, and scooped the smaller boy into his other arm. "Back to bed, you two."

Lorna stared after Cameron and his two sons, a wistful smile on her face. Since she was a teenager, she'd known she wanted to work with kids, but she'd started to believe she was not destined to have her own children.

Now there was a chance that one day she'd have a little boy with dark hair and blue eyes, just like Blair.

Chapter Six

The following day, Cameron drove Lorna to the apartment she shared with three other nurses on the outskirts of London so she could pack a bag. Then he dropped her at the hospital in time for afternoon visiting hours. Blair had texted to tell her where his room was.

She strode through the sliding doors into the space-age glass and chrome reception area of the military hospital. A huge silver Christmas tree stood under the glass-domed roof, decorated with blue and white baubles. Lorna skirted the tree and took the elevator to the correct floor.

As she approached Blair's open door, the rumble of male laughter sounded. Wearing loose sweatpants, a sweatshirt, and slippers, Blair was sitting in the chair beside his bed. The modern ergonomic chair looked far more comfortable than the plastic one he'd had to use in the field hospital.

He opened his arms when he saw her. "Lorna, love." His lips quirked in his usual smile and her heart gave a little kick. She'd spent a long night tossing and turning, wondering how he was. She leaned into his embrace, her eyelids drifting down as his lips brushed hers. How had she been friends with him for so long without kissing him? That seemed unbelievable now.

"Missed you," she whispered.

A man cleared his throat and she straightened to find Radley Knight seated on the other side of the room in the visitor's chair. She'd been so focused on Blair, she hadn't noticed he had company.

Radley was Cameron's older brother, and had often visited Kindrogan. He must be nearly forty now with a distinguished touch of gray at his temples. He'd always possessed a natural air of authority. He was so like his father, a senior army officer with the demeanor of a man who gave commands and expected them to be obeyed.

He rose and came towards her to kiss her on the cheek. "Hello, Lorna. It's been a long time."

"Radley, how are you?"

"Very well."

"Rad was just telling me he's been promoted to brigadier to oversee the new teaching wing of the hospital. It's a joint-forces facility for military doctors from all over the world. The flagship course will be Radley's pioneering limb-salvage techniques."

"A brigadier, wow. Congratulations. You're following in your father's footsteps," Lorna said.

"Thank you. I'm looking forward to the new challenge." He grinned, and for a moment he reminded her of the teenager he'd been, all those years ago during the long, lazy summers when he and Cameron visited Kindrogan.

"I was just telling Blair that his father wants him to travel to Scotland in an ambulance," Radley said.

"Not going to happen." Blair shook his head.

"Equally, I don't think you should use public transport." Radley picked up Blair's chart, examined it for a moment, and pressed his lips together. "You're healing well, but do take care of yourself."

"We can rent a car." Lorna hadn't driven for a while, but she was perfectly capable. She'd learned to drive on the private estate roads at Kindrogan when she was only fourteen. "If you don't mind me chauffeuring you home."

"That won't be necessary." Sir Robert Mackenzie strode into the room, Lady Mackenzie a few steps behind him. "If Blair doesn't require an ambulance, he'll travel back to Scotland in the car with us."

Lorna's heart crashed. She was looking forward to spending eight or nine hours traveling alone with Blair. They could talk with no interruptions and make plans for the future. But there was no way in a million years she'd spend that long cooped up in a car with Sir Robert.

Lady Mackenzie bustled over to Blair and hugged and kissed him.

Lorna sidled out of the way.

"I'd rather make my own way home," Blair said.

"That's silly, darling." Lady Mackenzie stroked back his hair. "We're driving home anyway. Why not come with us? It'll be fun."

Blair smiled, but it looked like an effort. "No, honestly. Thank you for the offer, but I want to leave as soon as possible. Remember, I have the children from the Heroes' Kids charity due to arrive at Kindrogan for their adventure weekend in a few days. I need to be there."

Sir Robert and Lady Mackenzie exchanged a dubious glance that nearly made Lorna laugh. She'd be willing to bet neither would show their face at Kindrogan until the children had left.

"Excuse me a moment, will you. It's time for me to stretch my legs." Blair rose gingerly, took a few steps, and held out his hand to Lorna.

She gripped it tightly, and they walked slowly out of the room.

"If you'll excuse me, Sir Robert, Lady Mackenzie, I have to start my rounds." Radley followed them out.

"Can I use the computer in your office?" Blair lowered his voice and glanced over his shoulder as he spoke to Radley.

"Certainly. I'll show you the way."

They stepped into the elevator, where Radley scanned a security pass to take them to the floor that housed the senior officers' private rooms and the operating suites.

When they reached Radley's office, Blair searched the Internet for a car-rental site and scrolled through the cars. "We'd better go for a four-wheel-drive. December in Scotland means lots of snow."

"Snow." Lorna shook her head as memories cascaded back: skiing, building snowmen, snowball fights. They'd had so much fun together when they were young.

Blair selected the biggest four-wheel-drive and booked it to be delivered to the hospital the following day.

"You're sure you don't want to travel with your parents?" she asked.

Blair gave a wry laugh, his hand pressed to his sore belly. "I love them, but they're unbearable together. Dad will criticize Mum for spending so much time in Barbados, and she'll accuse him of having an affair. Every time they're together, they blame each other for their relationship problems."

He rose and wrapped his arms around her. "Anyway, I want to spend the time with you. We can talk, and maybe stop off somewhere on the way to break the journey."

"Just remember," Radley said, "no driving or heavy lifting for six weeks. And don't do anything that will put a strain on your stomach." He raised his eyebrows meaningfully.

The drive to Scotland took longer than expected. Sitting

in the car made Blair's wound ache, so they had to stop frequently for him to walk and loosen up. They took the journey slowly and stopped halfway at a quaint country-house hotel in the Lake District.

Lorna enjoyed the easy conversation, reminiscing with Blair about their childhood, discussing what they would do when he was healed. Even the silences were comfortable. When Blair nodded off, Lorna glanced at him with a smile, feeling protective of this man she loved. She must be honest with him about the past, but that could wait until he was better.

During the journey, Blair received a text from Julia Braithwaite to say the French doctor had been rescued and brought to the field hospital. Blair and Lorna grinned at each other in relief. After being held captive, the sense of freedom was exhilarating.

On the second day of the journey, they met snow as they crossed the Scottish border. By the time they passed Edinburgh, huge, fluffy flakes pelted out of the sky, testing the windshield wipers to their limit. The vehicle's headlights came on automatically as the light level dropped, even though it was only midafternoon.

"If it carries on like this, the snow gate will close," Lorna said. At the entrance to the Kinder Valley, an automatic barrier lowered over the road when it was impassable. If the gate was down, they'd have to stay in a hotel for a night or two until the snowplows did their job.

Lorna bit her lip as she glanced at Blair. She was enjoying the journey, but Blair looked weary and he was obviously in pain. He needed to lie down and rest.

"I'll check the webcam on the website." Blair pulled out his phone.

Lorna concentrated as the weather worsened, a subtle tension filling her as Blair stared at his phone.

"The gate's still open," he announced.

They both fell silent, staring out at the white

landscape as they neared the snow gate. The falling flakes eased off and a ray of late-afternoon sunshine broke through the gray clouds. The familiar valley flanked by cloud-topped mountains lay before them, the rocks and pine trees clothed in a pristine coating of white. As they passed through the raised barrier of the snow gate, Lorna's breath whooshed out in relief.

"I'll call Duncan and tell him we're nearly there," Blair said.

Blair had a short conversation with his brother, smiling and laughing.

"He knows I'm coming, right?" Lorna asked.

"Of course. I called him from the hospital before we left. I warned him Mum and Dad probably won't be along until just before Christmas."

The lights of Kinder Vale gleamed under the gray sky. A lump formed in Lorna's throat as they passed the church, the doctor's surgery, the village hall, and the tiny primary school she'd attended. On the green outside the hall, a tall Christmas tree twinkled with colored lights, just as it had during her childhood.

Past the railway station, she drove up the steep hill and turned down the track onto Kindrogan Estate land. Even disguised by a blanket of snow, she remembered the route as if she'd come this way only yesterday.

"How many hundreds of times did we cycle this road?" Her voice came out thick with emotion.

Blair's warm hand settled on her knee and squeezed. "Happy times," he said.

Lorna's chest tightened as she shifted down a gear and they neared the top of the hill above Loch Kinder. She lifted her foot off the accelerator and the vehicle drifted to a halt.

Like a long-lost friend, Kindrogan Castle stood proudly at the head of the loch, light shining from its windows across the water, the majestic building crowned with distant snowy mountain peaks.

Tears tightened Lorna's chest and she pressed a hand over her mouth. How had she stayed away so long? This was her home, the place where she'd left her heart. She'd let Sir Robert drive her away with his cruel words, but she'd stayed away for so long to avoid her mother.

"Lorna, love. Are you all right?" Blair rubbed her shoulder.

"Yes." Her voice cracked on the word and she sucked in a breath to hold back the tears. "Thank you," she whispered.

"What for?"

"For bringing me home. Without you, I might never have come back." Happy memories swirled through her mind, all involving Blair. He was so intimately woven with her recollections of this place that he and Kindrogan were inseparable. Perhaps that was why she'd held herself back from admitting her feelings for him.

Loving Blair meant coming home in every sense of the word, and this was a bittersweet experience. Coming home meant facing up to the past that she'd shut out of her mind and denied for too long. Coming home meant finally finding out the truth.

It was time to visit her mother and face up to the terrible possibility that she had been the one to split up Blair's parents. Then Lorna would have to tell him. When she did, he might not feel quite the same way about her.

Blair's phone dinged and he glanced at the screen. "The snow gate has just closed. We're officially cut off from civilization."

He grinned at her and she grinned back conspiratorially. What was it about this place that made her feel like a mischievous child again?

She shifted into gear and moved off, the big black four-wheel-drive skidding as they went down the steep hill.

"We could do with snow chains," she said.

"I don't think they supply those for rental cars in Oxford."

They both laughed. There was something wild and untamed about Scotland—an elemental excitement that sang in her blood. Up here, away from civilization, anything was possible.

With her gaze trained on Kindrogan Castle, Lorna skirted the loch, watching as the colored lights of the Christmas tree in the dining room became visible through the window. A smile tugged at her lips. Christmas at Kindrogan had always been fun. Lots of presents under the tree, heaps of food, games, and music.

"Do you remember the time we nicked the whiskey out of your father's office and hid in the priest hole to try it?"

"Don't remind me."

They'd both been sick as dogs afterwards and missed their Christmas dinner.

Lorna drove around the castle and pulled up by the back door, as she'd done many times before. She released a breath she felt she'd been holding since the day she left.

The back door opened and Duncan's tall, solid silhouette filled the gap. A frisson of nerves passed through her. They hadn't exactly parted on good terms.

She opened her car door and slipped out. Hurrying around the vehicle, her shoes crunched through the snow. She held Blair's door wide for him to climb out, then offered him her arm.

He huffed. "This is emasculating. I should open the door for you."

"Stop complaining, Major Mackenzie. Let's go inside out of the cold."

They trod gingerly across the slippery ground

towards the door.

"Welcome home." Duncan strode out and grabbed their bags from the back of the vehicle then followed them inside.

Two Westies circled around their feet, barking and wagging their tails. "Meet Torrie and Bruce," Blair said. Lorna stooped to pat them, swallowing back a stab of sorrow. Dear old Bessie, the border collie who'd shared their childhood adventures, must be long gone.

"The wounded hero returns." Duncan grinned and carefully embraced Blair, patting him on the back. "Good to have you home. You had me worried there for a few days."

Lorna inhaled the familiar smell of old wood, beeswax polish, and something indefinable that was Kindrogan. She crouched to help Blair remove his snowy shoes, laughing as the dogs tried to assist, using the distraction to avoid Duncan's gaze for as long as possible. When she finally straightened and glanced his way, he smiled.

"Lorna. It's been too long. How are you?" Duncan sounded pleased to see her. That was a surprise.

"I'm fine. Apart from being kidnapped by rebel forces in Africa, of course. That put a bit of a crimp in things for a few days."

Duncan chuckled. She had to crane her neck to look up at him. He'd always been tall, but he'd filled out and was built like the side of a barn. She preferred Blair's lean, muscular physique. She always had.

A woman with long blonde hair came into the kitchen, a toddler in her arms. "Blair, we were worried you wouldn't make it tonight because of the weather. It's wonderful to see you." She came and kissed his cheek. "Those two days you were missing were awful."

"Lorna, this is Naomi, my wife." Duncan took the toddler from her arms and held the little girl up, jiggling her until she giggled. "And this little angel is our daughter, Holly."

"Lovely to meet you." Lorna shook Naomi's hand. Blair had told her Naomi used to be an army doctor as well. Now she worked part-time in the local hospital so she could spend time with Holly.

"I'll show you to your room. Duncan will bring up the bags." Naomi led the way out of the kitchen.

"Blair, remember you shouldn't lift anything." Lorna rested a hand on his arm before she followed Naomi.

As Lorna and Naomi mounted the stairs side by side, they chatted.

"Nothing's changed." Lorna took in the historic family portraits, the Mackenzie coat of arms over the front door, and the swords and shields decorating the wood-paneled walls.

"I forgot that Duncan said you know the place. You used to live in one of the estate cottages, didn't you?"

"That's right. My mum was the cleaner here."

"You were lucky to grow up in these surroundings. I love it here, and so does Holly. The little monkey has a thing for water. Just what we need when we have a huge drowning hazard right outside the door. We have to watch her like a hawk when she goes outside."

Lorna had been uncertain how she'd get along with Duncan's wife, but she felt immediately at ease with her.

"I wasn't sure if you'd want a room of your own, or if you'd share with Blair. I've put you in his sister's old room. If you don't want to use it, that's fine."

"Thanks." Lorna peered into the cozy interior of what used to be Megan's bedroom. "To be honest, I'm not sure myself." She glanced along the corridor and lowered her voice. "Blair and I have only just started dating."

"Oh." Naomi's eyebrows rose. "From what Duncan said, I thought you'd known each other forever."

"We have. It's a bit complicated."

"Mummy, Mummy, Mummy." The happy chatter of Naomi's little girl sounded nearby. The toddler appeared at the top of the stairs, obviously having negotiated them on all fours. She stood up and scampered towards them.

Naomi swept the child into her arms with a grin and kissed her. "Where's that daddy of yours, sweetie?"

Duncan appeared with a bag in each hand, and set Lorna's at her feet. "Your luggage, ma'am."

They all turned and waited as Blair hobbled along the corridor, a pained expression on his face. "Sitting too long in a car makes everything hurt."

Lorna checked her watch. "Did you take your painkillers?"

"A moment ago."

"Lie down for a while and rest before dinner," Duncan said. "Doctor's orders."

"I'm planning to." Blair stopped beside them and frowned at the open door to Megan's bedroom. "Why are we looking this room?"

"I thought I might sleep in here." Lorna's cheeks heated at the frown on Blair's face. Last night at the hotel, she'd asked for separate rooms because Blair was in pain and needed a good night's sleep. They should have discussed the sleeping arrangements at Kindrogan, but somehow the subject hadn't come up.

Blair extended a hand to Lorna. "I've spent ten years dreaming of you. Now you're mine, I want to be with you, darling."

A burst of pleasure wiped away her uncertainty. She slipped her fingers in his and they continued along the corridor.

Chapter Seven

Blair led Lorna into his bedroom, his insides churning in turmoil. He shouldn't press her to share his room if she wanted her own space. He paused and leaned a hand on the wardrobe, hanging his head. "I'm sorry, love. Of course you can sleep in Megan's room if you'd rather."

Her hand slipped out of his and his heart sank, but she didn't walk away as he expected; she moved in front of him and laid both palms on his chest. "I want to be with you. It's just early days, and I'm not sure what you're expecting."

Blair wrapped his arms around her and buried his face in the sweet curve of her neck. "I want to fall asleep holding your hand. When I wake in the night, I want you there so I know this isn't a dream. That you really do love me."

Of course he wanted more than that eventually, when he was fit and Lorna was ready to take things further. But for now, knowing she was with him in his bed would help him rest easier.

She rose on tiptoes and pressed her lips to his. "Oh, Blair. I love you, darling. Don't ever doubt it." Her fingers skimmed up his neck and into his hair, making his eyes close at the blissful sensation of her touch.

"Let's get you into bed for a rest," she whispered.

"Good idea." Every muscle in Blair's body ached; he was so exhausted. He'd been tense the whole journey, trying to hold his body still so his belly didn't hurt.

Lorna led him across the room and turned back the bedcovers. Blair sat on the edge of the bed and gazed around at the old dark-wood furniture, the sporting trophies, the band posters, and the photos, wondering what she thought of this room—a shrine to a happy childhood. The décor had barely changed since she was last here.

She wandered to the chest of drawers and picked up a photo in a silver frame. "I remember when we climbed to the top of the tree and Duncan took this photo. Your father was so upset with us." Lorna laughed, a carefree warble that Blair hadn't heard for years—not since Duncan decided to date her and screwed everything up.

Blair had been furious with his brother for trying to steal her, even though Blair had never asked her out because of their age difference. That had been his wake up call—the first time he understood his feelings for her were more than friendship.

His father had gone crazy back then, shouting at Lorna's mother. After that he sent Mrs. Bell and Lorna away. But his father's overreaction and his parents' estrangement had eclipsed his anger at his brother. The trouble between his parents had actually drawn him closer to his siblings.

Blair frowned and rubbed his eyes. He still didn't know what had gone on that day. It was weird, because right after that his mother left for Barbados.

Duncan knocked on the door and brought in their bags. "Settle in and we'll see you at eight for dinner. Remember, the Heroes' Kids charity group is arriving in three days."

"Yeah, I know." The charity was his brainchild, and very close to his heart. Blair had been looking forward to hosting a trip for the kids of servicemen who'd lost their lives. Getting shot had really messed with his plans.

Duncan rested a hand on Blair's shoulder. "Don't worry. We have everything in hand."

"Thank you. I'll do what I can to help."

"No, you'll rest and recover, laddie." Duncan raised his eyebrows in his "I'm the older brother so you'll do what I say" look.

"Okay."

Blair ran his fingers inside the waistband of his sweatpants. They were loose, but after sitting in the car for so many hours, they pinched his wound. He was bone weary and the dull ache from his abdomen throbbed through his torso and down his legs. All he wanted to do was lie down.

Duncan left the room, closing the door softly behind him.

"You need some sleep, love," Lorna said. "I can see you're hurting. Aren't the pain meds working?"

"I don't know. Maybe the last dose hasn't kicked in yet."

While Lorna unzipped her bag, Blair pulled off his sweatpants and slid beneath the covers. His breath rushed out in relief to be lying flat in a soft bed.

Lorna fiddled with her folded clothes, obviously not sure what to do next.

"Will you get in bed and give me a cuddle?" he asked.

"Of course." Lorna toed off her sneakers, pulled the thick pullover off over her head, and slid under the covers beside him. She snuggled close and he pressed his nose to her hair, breathing in the wonderful fragrance of her. If he could sleep by her side for the rest of his life, he'd be a happy man.

His gaze moved to his bedside cabinet, to the top drawer. In the back corner was a small blue velvet box that contained a diamond ring. Ten years ago he'd been desperate to impress her, and he'd blown all his savings on that ring. He'd been so hopeful, so naive and stupid, proposing to her as soon as he turned twenty, a few weeks after his father sent her away. He shouldn't have been surprised she threw the ring back in his face.

Could you offer a girl the same ring twice? Perhaps that would be bad luck. He should wait until he was healed and propose somewhere romantic. Yet even as he imagined a candlelit dinner, soft music, and going down on one knee, he was already boosting himself up on his elbow to reach into the drawer. Pain shot from his wound through his body, and he gritted his teeth.

"Blair, what're you doing?" Lorna sat up and frowned. "If you want something, let me get it for you." Lorna's fingers stroked the hair off his forehead, and she kissed him.

Blair lowered himself back on the bed and closed his eyes, waiting for the ache in his belly to subside. He just wanted to get the marriage proposal over with and put his ring on her finger.

Lorna stood on Kinder Flat with her arm around Blair, the cold wind whistling down from the mountains and stinging her cheeks. Blair leaned against the side of the Kindrogan Estate Land Rover as they watched an Air Sea Rescue helicopter flying in beneath the steely gray clouds.

The first treat of the kids' long weekend break was this helicopter ride. It had been easy to organize as Blair's family was heavily involved with the local mountain rescue group, and they had a good relationship with the Royal Navy Air Sea Rescue.

Lorna squinted as the huge yellow Sea King sank towards the ground, the rotor blades throwing up a hurricane of snow from the flat cement area where the helicopter normally landed to pick up the mountain rescue team.

Old Angus, the Mackenzie family gillie who had worked on the estate supervising the hunting and fishing since before Lorna was born, climbed out of the Land Rover, pulled his hat low, and scowled as the helicopter set down.

"You ready to help organize some games for the kids?" Lorna asked Angus. He glared at her in response. He was renowned for being grumpy, but he had always watched out for them when they were young. He'd even told fibs to Sir Robert to keep them out of trouble.

"I dinnae want them here at all. All this extra work just before Christmas." Angus grumbled to himself as he limped to the back of the vehicle and pulled open the door, ready for the passengers. Blair shared a chuckle with Lorna. They both knew Angus's bark was worse than his bite.

Blair's youngest brother, Hew, was also there with a vehicle. After the helicopter touched down, he jogged over to it and helped open the door and lift the children down. Eight kids between nine and twelve scurried towards them, the downdraft from the helicopter making them duck and squeal as they ran.

Two young soldiers, who'd volunteered to assist, also jumped out of the Sea King and helped unload the kids' bags.

"Hello, lads and lasses," Blair called as they approached. "Hope you had a good flight."

"Hi, Major Mackenzie." The three girls and five boys all gathered around him, grinning and fidgeting with excitement.

"No formalities. You're on vacation. You can call me Blair and this is Lorna." He put his hand on her shoulder. "You climb in this Land Rover, and your bags can go in the other one."

"Let's help the kids climb in," he said, beckoning the

group to the back of the vehicle.

Blair had rested for the last three days and he was in less pain now, but Lorna was determined to make sure he didn't overdo things.

"I'll do the helping." Lorna moved in front of him and offered a hand to the children as they stepped up. Bundled in thick coats, hats, and gloves, they squashed into the back of the Land Rover, chattering.

When they were all settled, Angus slammed the door and hopped in the driver's seat. Hew had loaded the bags in the other vehicle and was talking to the two soldiers who'd come to help. Lorna and Blair climbed into the front of the Land Rover, and they drove the mile along the private estate road to the castle, Hew following behind.

Over the next four days, Kindrogan Castle became a hive of activity, with children dashing about, shouting, and having fun. Lorna fell into bed exhausted every night after supervising hikes, games, and playing in the snow. Blair was frustrated he couldn't do more, but she and all his family made sure he was careful.

His sister and her husband, Megan and Daniel Fabian, took the children to Glenshee ski resort a few miles away, and gave the kids skiing and snowboarding lessons. Hew took them on a Land Rover safari around the estate, spotting winter wildlife. Lyall Stewart, the local policeman and leader of the Kindrogan Mountain Rescue group, taught them how to stay safe in the cold weather.

On the final evening of the children's vacation, everyone gathered around the huge table in the dining room at Kindrogan Castle for an early Christmas dinner. Lorna and Naomi had prepared the dinner while Megan set the table and wrapped a small gift for each child to go under the Christmas tree. The men kept the children busy, playing party games.

Much later, stuffed with turkey and Christmas

pudding, Lorna sat with Holly cuddled on her lap while the visiting kids crowded around Blair, pleading with him to tell them about being taken prisoner by the rebel troops.

Blair had that indefinable quality of charisma that attracted people. He was a handsome man, but it was more than looks. He smiled and gestured with his hands, radiating energy and enthusiasm no matter what he talked about. The children were drawn to him, just like the people in the refugee camp had been. Just like Lorna was.

In the festive lights, his dark hair shone, and his blue eyes twinkled as he embellished the tale with all sorts of excitement to make the children gasp, their eyes as wide as saucers. The fact he'd been shot and survived made him even more of a hero in their eyes, especially as they had all lost their fathers.

Holly snuggled closer to Lorna, poking her thumb in her mouth. She blinked her adorable blue eyes sleepily. "Are you ready for your bed, sweetie?"

Lorna smoothed back the little girl's fine blonde hair; her heart pinched with longing. Naomi had explained how she'd found Holly abandoned when she was a newborn. Lorna envied Naomi, secretly wishing she'd been the one to find this little angel. In the last few days, she'd fallen in love with her. Lorna's biological clock was ticking, and she longed for her own son or daughter.

"Holly's bedtime, I'm afraid," Duncan whispered.

Lorna didn't want to part with her. Instead of passing the child over, she rose and walked out into the hall with Duncan. At the bottom of the stairs, she relinquished her hold on the bundle of joy and let him have her.

"You have a lucky daddy. Good night, sweetie." Lorna kissed Holly's cheek then stepped back with a sigh.

"You'll have your own baby one day." Duncan smiled sympathetically.

"Perhaps." She and Blair had other hurdles to leap first.

"By the way, I saw your mother in the village yesterday. She's the caretaker at a holiday cottage complex farther down the valley. She wants you to visit while you're here."

Shock pulsed through Lorna, and it took her a moment to calm herself. Having the kids here on vacation had proved a good way to push her mother to the back of her mind. But she couldn't put off a visit forever. They had talked on the phone occasionally over the last ten years, but Lorna had not come face to face with her since the terrible fight over her mother's relationship with Sir Robert.

"Are you all right? You look very pale."

"I'm fine, Duncan." Lorna turned away as he went up the stairs with Holly in his arms. She pressed her fingers to her temples to massage away the stress. At the door to the dining room she paused, a smile pulling at her lips to see the children gathered around Blair.

Ten years ago, she'd walked away from the emotional quagmire her mother and Sir Robert had created. If she wanted a future with Blair, there was no running away this time.

Chapter Eight

Blair pulled the blue velvet box out of his bedside table drawer, flipped up the lid, and checked the ring. The oval diamond twinkled at him. Pressing his lips together, he firmed his resolve.

Over the last few days while the children were here, he'd had no private time to arrange a romantic dinner so he could propose. Then last night Lorna suggested they go out for lunch and visit her mother today, giving Blair the perfect opportunity to ask her to marry him.

He'd booked a table for lunch at a nice restaurant in Braemar. On the way back to Kinder Vale, they could stop at the viewpoint over the loch, share a few kisses, and he would pop the question. Then Lorna could break the news to her mother when they visited in the afternoon.

Blair had hidden a bottle of champagne and two glasses in the rental car earlier. The comfortable four-wheel-drive with its reclining leather seats was more modern than the estate Land Rovers. The luxury vehicle was an ideal place to relax and admire the view after their meal, an ideal place to ask Lorna to be his wife.

Closing the ring box, Blair slipped it in his jacket pocket. His heart already pounded with nerves. He couldn't shake his strange sense of foreboding, which was crazy when he and Lorna were getting along so well.

"Blair, are you ready?" Her voice came from downstairs.

He strode along the corridor, his abdominal injury much improved. Rest and a comfortable bed helped a lot.

"I'm coming," he shouted as he trod down the stairs.

With her blonde hair in its usual braid, Lorna was wrapped in her pink coat and scarf, a hat and gloves in her hand. She smiled as he approached, but tense lines beside her eyes and mouth strengthened his sense of foreboding.

"Is something troubling you, love?"

She flashed him an overly bright grin. "Of course not."

Her denial of the obvious only served to worry him more. Perhaps it was the prospect of spending Christmas with his father that worried her. Maybe Blair should wait to propose until after the holiday when they left here? He considered his options as he followed her through the kitchen and out the back door.

His parents were due to arrive on Christmas Eve, and it was quite possible they might object to his plans. After all, when Duncan wanted to date Lorna, for some unknown reason his father had thrown a fit. Blair wanted his ring on her finger before his father tossed a monkey wrench into the works.

He strode past her and opened her car door. She smiled, pressed a kiss to his lips, and climbed in. Gradually as he healed, things were returning to the way they should be. He wished he could drive, but he wouldn't go against doctor's orders.

Lorna started the engine, and the vehicle glided along the loch road, then headed through Kinder Vale. They took the mountain pass to Braemar. It hadn't snowed for a couple of days, so the road was still clear after the last pass by the snowplow.

The majestic snowy mountains stretched out as far as the eye could see, a beautiful but dangerous landscape, safe viewed from inside a vehicle, but deadly for the unwary who tried to take it on without training and safety gear.

Lorna drove into the small Scottish town of Braemar, and turned into the car park beside the Thistle. Inside the restaurant, they were shown to a private table in a nook beside the huge fireplace.

A Christmas tree sparkled nearby while chains of colorful foil decorations draped the thick wooden beams in the ceiling and around the fireplace. The crackling fire, soft music, and the murmur of conversation gave the place a cozy, welcoming feel.

The traditional Scottish dishes all sounded delicious. Lorna chose chicken in the heather, made with Scottish heather honey, while Blair selected roast Scottish lamb with black pudding and apple stuffing.

Despite the tasty meal, Blair had little appetite. He wanted the uncertainty over with so he and Lorna could get on with their future.

As they wandered back to the car hand in hand, Lorna seemed distant and distracted again.

"Are you okay, love?"

She flashed him a smile. "Yes, fine. Just thinking about how long it's been since I last saw Mum."

They climbed in the car and headed back down the mountain road. "Pull over at the viewpoint." Blair pointed to the turnoff that led to a parking area. They'd stopped here numerous times when they were younger to hike along the ridge so they could look down on Kindrogan Castle.

Lorna frowned but did as he asked. She halted the vehicle, giving them an uninterrupted view over Loch Kinder and Kindrogan Estate land.

Blair's breath rushed out in awe at the magnificent

view. It was easy to take his home for granted, but spending time away helped him appreciate the natural beauty.

"Amazing," Lorna said. "I'd forgotten how spectacular it is here. Or maybe I'd put it out of my mind on purpose."

"Why would you do that?"

She angled her head as if thinking, but didn't answer.

Her strange mood was really getting to him. "Please tell me what's wrong."

"Did you know I haven't seen Mum since I left Scotland?"

"Of course." He'd suggested she return home with him many times over the last ten years, but she never would. She must have more on her mind than her mum.

"Be honest with me, Lorna. Is there a problem between us?"

She turned to him then, concern in her eyes. "Oh, no. Of course not." She leaned over the gearshift and wrapped her arms around his neck. "I love you, Blair Mackenzie. Whatever happens, always remember that."

Her words were obviously meant to reassure him; they did the opposite. "What do you mean, 'whatever happens'?"

She shook her head, a pained expression on her face. "Don't worry about it."

Now he was even more worried. This was not the time to propose, but the ring was burning a hole in his pocket. He didn't want to take it home again.

"Lorna."

"Yes?"

Blair pulled the blue velvet box out of his jacket pocket and flipped up the lid to reveal the small gold band set with a diamond, the symbol of his love, the symbol of all his hopes and dreams for the future. His heart thundered in his chest. "I love you, Lorna Bell. Will you do me the honor of becoming my wife?"

Shock startled Lorna out of her distracting thoughts. Blair's proposal took her completely by surprise. She'd had no idea he was planning to pop the question today. How could she accept his ring when in a few hours he might ask for it back?

She desperately wanted to say yes, let him slip this beautiful diamond on her finger, and pretend everything was perfect. But she couldn't.

"No. Not yet. Ask me later." She wrapped both her hands around his, trying to close the lid of the ring box.

For a few moments, the painful turmoil of her thoughts consumed her. Too late she considered how he must feel. She tried to smile, to soften the blow of her response, but Blair stared at her, slack-jawed with shock, the pain in his eyes like a slap across her face.

Then his expression hardened, his jaw clenching. He recoiled from her, jerking his hands from her grip.

He swiveled in his seat and grabbed the door handle. "This damn ring is cursed."

Lorna stared in horror as he shoved open the car door and started to climb out, the ring box clenched in a fist.

"Blair, wait!" Lorna scrambled out into the snow, slipping on the slick ground as she dashed around the front of the vehicle. She reached him just in time to grab his sleeve as he raised his hand.

He tried to pitch the ring over the cliff, but Lorna dragged down his arm. The tiny box fell ten yards away, bounced across the icy rocks, and landed in a pocket of snow on the edge of the precipice.

Lorna's breath sawed in and out as she scrambled over rocks to retrieve the ring, soaking her trousers and sleeves in the snow.

"Lorna, come back. Don't be silly. It's slippery." The

angry tone of Blair's voice changed to concern as she neared the sheer drop. But even in her frantic rush to rescue this precious ring, she wasn't about to put her life at risk. She knew this piece of cliff, knew the rocks were solid. There was no loose shale to come away under her feet. As long as she took it carefully, and didn't slip on the ice, she'd be fine.

Blair called her name again, a note of panic in his voice. She tuned him out, focused on where she placed her feet and hands, her target the patch of snow where the ring box had disappeared.

She pulled off her glove and dug her hand into the soft snow. Heart pounding with relief, her trembling fingers closed around the wet velvet. She pushed the box into the pocket of her coat and made sure the Velcro closure was fastened before carefully making her way back to safety.

"What the hell were you thinking?" Blair shouted as she reached flat ground and brushed snow off her clothes. "You could have fallen to your death."

Now the ring was safely in her pocket, Lorna's own temper fired up. "What the hell were *you* thinking? That was a crazy thing to do."

"The ring's jinxed."

Lorna shook her head in bewilderment.

"You've turned it down twice."

"I didn't turn it down. I asked you to wait until later."

He shook his head firmly. "You said no. I'm not deaf."

"I said no. Not now. Ask me later."

Blair threw his hands in the air, turned away, then back again. "I didn't hear all that. I stopped listening at no."

Lorna stepped closer, flattened her palms on his chest, and rubbed to soothe his injured pride. Her heart was tight with pain to think she'd hurt him again. That was the last thing she wanted to do. "Blair, I love you. Of course I want to marry you."

He blinked at her, confusion written across his face. "Then why not just say yes?"

"If you still want to marry me after we've talked to Mum, then I'll gladly accept."

Lines gathered on Blair's forehead. "What on earth has your mum got to do with us getting engaged?"

Lorna had held back from sharing her suspicions with Blair and agonized over them in private, trying to spare him the trauma while he was recovering. If there was the slightest chance she was wrong, she didn't want him to worry about nothing. But it wasn't fair to keep him in the dark any longer, especially after what had just happened.

Lorna pressed her forehead to Blair's chest for a moment to summon her courage. Wetting her lips, she raised her head and met his gaze. "I think my mum had an affair with your father."

Blair shook his head emphatically. "No way."

His dad having an affair with the cleaner? That was ridiculous. His father had been against Duncan dating Lorna because she was the cleaner's daughter.

Blair cast back ten years and examined his memories of the time. Sally Bell was a very attractive woman who'd lost her husband at a young age. She'd spent a lot of time at Kindrogan, even when she wasn't working. At the time, Blair had been happy because it meant Lorna was at Kindrogan as well.

His father had definitely liked Sally Bell, but his mother hadn't been such a fan. She'd called her a flirt and complained that she took liberties, treating Kindrogan Castle as if she lived there.

A hint of doubt burgeoned until it filled Blair's thoughts. Seemingly innocuous memories from his past assumed new, more sinister meanings. Things that had

71

confused him now became clear. "No." He closed his eyes, his fist clenched against his thigh.

"I didn't mention it before, because I'm not absolutely certain. I might have this all wrong." Lorna laid her hand on his arm. Without thinking, he stepped away from her touch. Right now he couldn't bear the contact.

"Let's go and ask her." Blair climbed in the car and snapped on his seat belt. Every muscle in his body clenched, desperate for the truth. He didn't want to talk; he didn't even want to think. He just wanted to know the truth.

With a worried glance his way, Lorna rounded the vehicle and climbed in. She backed up then turned onto the road. In uncomfortable silence, they drove the narrow roads through Kinder Vale and along the valley in the opposite direction from Kindrogan.

When Blair's mother accused his father of having an affair, Blair had wondered if she suspected something had happened in London. It had never occurred to him that his dad was carrying on with Sally Bell, right here at Kindrogan under his mother's nose.

His poor mum. Blair swiped a hand over his face, remorse and anger crowding his mind. None of them had taken her complaints seriously. They all thought she was the one being difficult when she packed up and moved to the family villa in Barbados. His father had accused her of having a midlife crisis when it was him at fault.

At the end of a stony track, a wooden gate stood open. A snow-topped sign that read Black Crag Farm Cottages pointed towards a yard surrounded by old barns that had been converted into holiday accommodations. Blinking Christmas lights trimmed the cottage porches and a decorated tree stood in a stone cattle trough that had been turned into a flower planter.

This must be the place where Mrs. Bell worked. The atmosphere in the vehicle crackled with tension as Lorna pulled up and cut the engine.

"Here we are," she said softly.

Blair just grunted. Right now, his mind was too preoccupied for speech.

They climbed out and checked the small wooden name plaques outside each cottage. At the far end was one that said caretaker's cottage.

Lorna led the way and knocked on the door. Blair trailed a few steps behind, his hands shoved into his pockets. After a few moments, the lock clicked and the door opened.

"Lorna! You came." Sally Bell looked a little older, but she was still an attractive woman with shoulder-length blonde hair and blue eyes. It was obvious why Blair's father had been tempted.

She and Lorna hugged each other, then Mrs. Bell turned to Blair with a flirty smile. "Blair Mackenzie. My, you've grown up to be just as handsome as Sir Robert." She tried to hug him, but he stepped back out of reach. He couldn't pretend to be friendly when her words stoked his anger.

"Did you have an affair with my father?"

Mrs. Bell's eyes widened. She stared at him unblinking for a moment, before her gaze moved to Lorna.

"Please don't say it's none of my business, this time, Mum. We need to know," Lorna said more gently.

"Can't we talk about this over a cup of tea?" Sally Bell turned and disappeared down the corridor. Lorna followed. With a frustrated sigh, Blair went after them.

A breakfast bar divided the small sitting room from the kitchen. Lorna's mother bustled about, filling the kettle with water, and setting cups on saucers. Blair had no patience with all this time wasting.

"It's a simple question, Mrs. Bell. I'd like a simple

answer. Did you have an affair with my father?"

Her cheeks flushed and she avoided his gaze. "It ended a long time ago."

Pain, anger, and contempt raced through Blair until he could barely contain the emotional turmoil. "Would that be ten years ago? About the time my mother walked out on us?"

Mrs. Bell's cheeks went bright red, tears filling her eyes. "I'm sorry, Blair. I never meant to hurt anyone."

Blair pivoted away, pain shooting from his wound at the sudden motion, but the discomfort was nothing compared to the crashing torrent of anguish almost blinding him. He strode along the corridor, out of the front door, and towards the road.

He needed to get away from that woman who'd ruined his parents' relationship and destroyed his family. Because of her, his mother had walked out. Blair had been twenty when she left, but he'd still missed her. Megan and Hew had been younger and it affected them more.

Stooping, he grabbed a stone from the edge of the road, and hurled it into the nearby river with a grunt of effort. If he threw a million stones, he would not get rid of this restless, furious energy that threatened to tear him apart. Striding on, he dragged in some deep breaths and blew them out, trying to calm down and get a hold of his temper.

Of course, it took two to tango. His father was just as much to blame, but Sally Bell had always flirted with him. She'd probably led him on, hoping to get her feet under the laird's table. No wonder his father had flown off the handle when Lorna started dating Duncan. Like mother, like daughter.

Hell. That wasn't fair. Lorna was nothing like her mother. Blair scraped his hand back through his hair, his feelings a tangled mess of confusion.

Chapter Nine

"Blair!" Lorna turned to go after him, but her mother grabbed her arm.

"Give him some time to think."

Lorna stared down the corridor as Blair slammed the front door behind him. Her heart drummed so loudly it echoed in her ears. This was her worst nightmare come true. He must be terribly upset. At least she had given him a little warning by telling him earlier. It turned out that *had* been the right thing to do.

Her mother released her. Without consciously deciding to move, Lorna's feet took her after Blair. She pulled open the front door, stepped into the yard, and gazed around, searching for him. She caught a glimpse as he disappeared from view along the road.

Maybe he planned to walk home? But it was a long way when he was still healing. Perhaps she should go after him right away and pick him up?

"Come back and have your cup of tea. Give him time to get used to the idea." Her mother's voice came from the kitchen.

Heaving a sigh, Lorna returned inside and perched on a stool at the breakfast bar, fidgety and restless. She wanted desperately to talk to Blair and find out what he was thinking.

Lorna rested her head in her hands and closed her

eyes. This was horrible. Blair must be hurting terribly. She could have spared him if she'd kept her distance from him and never returned to Kindrogan. She'd done that for ten years and it had obviously been the right thing to do. The truth should have been left in the past.

A cup and saucer slid under her nose. She lifted her head and took a sip of tea.

"I heard Blair was shot," her mother said. "Those rebel soldiers didn't hurt you, did they?"

Lorna shook her head. That episode in Africa felt like it was from a different lifetime. So much had happened since then. If only she could go back in time, back to being just friends with Blair. She'd been wise to keep her emotions in check all these years. Now she would probably lose him completely.

"I was interviewed by the local paper when you were taken captive. I was quite the celebrity for a few days." Lorna's mother spoke with a jaunty tone that grated across Lorna's shredded nerves.

"If you'd been held prisoner for a couple more days, I think one of the national newspapers might have approached me."

"Are you serious, Mum?" Her mother actually sounded disappointed to have had her moment of fame cut short.

Her mother frowned. "Don't get wound up about every little thing I say. Your trouble is you take life too seriously."

"Blair was shot! We could have both been killed. That's about as serious as it gets." Anger shot up Lorna's spine. She sat ramrod straight, remembering numerous times when her mother had put herself first, including the obvious one that had caused their furious row and estrangement ten years ago, and now might ruin her relationship with Blair.

"How could you have an affair with Sir Robert when you knew he had a wife and children?"

"Don't speak to me like that. You have no idea what it was like trying to raise you alone. Sometimes I needed a man's help, and Robert was always there for me. One thing led to another. It wasn't my fault."

Lorna rubbed her temples as her head throbbed with a tension headache. She couldn't sit here doing nothing any longer. "I'm going to make sure Blair's all right."

Her mother shrugged. "If you chase him, he'll run away. You have to play hard to get."

"Oh, for goodness' sake. He was shot in the abdomen a few days ago and he's trying to walk ten miles back to Kindrogan. This has nothing to do with chasing him."

Lorna gave her mother a perfunctory hug but her heart wasn't in it. Her heart was as numb as if the chilly wind off the mountains blew right through her.

"Don't leave it so long next time," her mother said as she walked with her to the front door.

"No, Mum." Right now Lorna never wanted to see her again, but that would change when she calmed down.

Lorna headed to the vehicle, climbed in, and backed up, raising a hand to acknowledge her mother before she drove away.

A mile down the road she caught up with Blair, striding along as if he were in a race. As she drew level with him, she lowered the window. "Let me give you a ride back to Kindrogan."

He glanced at her but kept walking.

"Come on, Blair. It's a long way home."

He halted suddenly. Lorna pulled up and he climbed in. She released a breath loaded with relief. Now he was safely in the vehicle, she could take him home where he had Duncan to talk to.

Silence filled the car like a weight pressing down on her. There was no tension between them now; there was nothing. It was as if he'd thrown up a wall to block her out. He was there beside her, but he was a million miles away. She wanted to reach out to touch him but didn't dare.

It was a relief when Kindrogan Castle came into view. Blair unfastened his seat belt before they reached the back door. He climbed out of the car the moment it stopped moving. Without a word, he strode off towards the loch.

Lorna cut the engine and rested her forehead on the steering wheel. She felt as though someone had punched a hole through her chest and left a huge aching gap. Blair loved her; she knew that. Ten years of devotion didn't disappear this quickly. But in his mind she would forever be linked with the breakup of his parents. How would he cope with that?

The bump in Lorna's pocket reminded her of the precious cargo within. She dug out the velvet box and raised the lid. The pretty gold band and oval diamond sparkled in the light. She pulled the ring out and slipped it on the third finger of her left hand. It fit perfectly, as if it had been made for her.

Tears overflowed her lashes and ran down her cheeks. Life was so unfair. What Sir Robert and her mother did all those years ago had probably ruined any chance she and Blair had of finding happiness.

Lorna pulled off the ring, pushed it back in the velvet, and shut the box. Wiping away her tears, she climbed out and made her way to the back door.

As she went inside, Naomi was cutting up vegetables at the kitchen counter while Duncan sat on a chair at the table beside Holly in her high chair. She was banging her cup on the tray while Duncan tried to get a spoon in her mouth.

"Lorna, what's the matter?" Naomi reached her side in a moment, wiping her hands on a dishtowel before she put an arm around her shoulders. "Did you and

Blair argue?"

A sob tore from Lorna's throat before she could press a hand over her mouth.

"Is Blair all right?" Duncan demanded.

"No. He needs you. He went towards the loch." Lorna should probably warn Duncan what was wrong, but she had already summoned the anger of one Mackenzie brother today. She couldn't break this damning news to another.

Blair's thoughts circled around and around in his head, analyzing past events, trying to identify signs that had suggested all was not well between his parents. There had been plenty of clues; he just hadn't noticed because he was so wrapped up in his own life.

He gazed across the glassy surface of Loch Kinder in the fading light. Lacy patterns of ice fringed the water's edge. Mist drifted down off the pine-clad slopes to gather in dips and hollows, and his breath grew steamy as the temperature dropped.

If he'd known what was going on back then, could he have done anything about it? If he'd spoken to his father, might he have stopped the affair and kept his mother at home?

Duncan's even, solid footsteps crunched the pebbles as he approached. Blair's brother sat on the rock beside him and rubbed his hands together to warm them. "Lorna said you needed me."

Blair thought for a moment and nodded. "Yes." Lorna was right. Duncan's grounded common sense was exactly what he did need right now to help him make sense of his thoughts.

"So, did you two have an argument?" Duncan asked.

"No." If only it were that simple.

Duncan sighed. "Do I need to pull rank to get more than a monosyllabic answer?"

Blair turned up his collar and hunched into his

quilted, duck-down jacket. He wanted to talk about this, but it was difficult. In the end, the need to unburden himself won out. In halting sentences, he described the visit with Lorna's mother.

Once he started talking, he couldn't stop. Thinking aloud, he analyzed events from the past, things that had happened between Sally Bell and their father, things their mother had said, and his guilt for dismissing his mother's complaints.

He talked for what felt like hours. By the time he ran out of words, darkness had slipped down the glen like a thief stealing the daylight. In the far distance, the tiny lights of Kinder Vale twinkled as if nothing were wrong.

They sat in silence, the only sound the hoot of an owl, and the faint crackle of the ice on the gently moving water. Eventually, Duncan sucked in a deep breath and blew it out. "I guessed there was something between Dad and Sally."

"What? Why didn't you do anything about it?"

"I didn't know at the time. I worked it out later, after Dad sent Lorna away. I spent a long time wondering what Dad had against her." Duncan turned to face him, the lights from the castle catching his eyes. "He told me it wasn't acceptable for me to take advantage of a member of staff." He shook his head. "I wasn't, so that never made sense to me."

"It makes more sense now we know what he was up to."

"Precisely," Duncan said.

"Why didn't you tell me?"

Duncan shrugged. "It was in the past. There was nothing any of us could do to help."

"Do Meg and Hew know?"

"No, and I'd like to keep it that way."

That made sense. Why dump this on the others and make them feel bad?

"Have you talked to Lorna about it?" Duncan asked.

"No. Since I found out, I've been trying to get my head around it. She already knew. I get the impression she's suspected for years."

"Maybe, but she's pretty upset."

"Is she?" The thought of Lorna alone and distressed sent a jolt of remorse through him. He hadn't given her much thought since he found out. The affair was no surprise to her and she must be used to the idea. He was the ignorant one who'd not noticed what was right under his nose back then.

"She was crying when she came inside," Duncan said.

Blair closed his eyes and pinched the bridge of his nose. He'd been overwhelmed trying to come to terms with the revelation, and shut Lorna out completely. That hadn't been fair. Especially when he knew she was uncertain of his reaction.

"I tried to propose earlier and she turned me down. She seemed to think I might not want to marry her once I knew about the affair."

Duncan gripped Blair's arm. "Don't let what Dad did ruin your future. If you and Lorna want to get married, then do it."

For the first time since Sally Bell had admitted the affair, a glimmer of hope filtered through Blair's thoughts. Her revelation had cast a dark cloud over his hopes and dreams. Now Duncan's words lifted the darkness.

"Won't it be awkward for Mum and Dad, considering the past?"

"They'll get used to the idea. Don't punish yourself for Dad's mistakes."

The small glimmer of hope flared brighter. "I'll go and talk to Lorna."

As Lorna packed her clothes in her bag, Naomi stood watching at the door to Blair's bedroom, an anxious frown on her face. "I really can't see why you have to leave," she said for the umpteenth time.

Lorna hadn't explained the issue. It was Mackenzie dirty laundry and not her secret to spread around. Duncan could tell his wife.

"Blair obviously doesn't want to talk to me right now. I need to give him some space."

"I don't understand what's so terrible that you feel you have to leave."

It was a terrible revelation, but was it really so serious that Blair would break off their relationship? Before they spoke to Lorna's mother, their parents' affair felt like the end of the world. Now the secret was out in the open, it didn't seem as awful. As if the fear of it coming out had been worse than the reality. But Blair might not agree.

She wished they could discuss it, but he hadn't said a single word to her since her mother's confession.

Swallowing back more tears, Lorna pasted on a smile for Naomi's sweet little daughter. Holly toddled back and forth between the bedroom and the bathroom, bringing cosmetics and toiletries for Lorna to pack.

"That's not mine, angel. That belongs to Uncle Blair." Despite Lorna's misery, Holly's dear little face still warmed her heart. She would miss Holly very much, and she'd mourn losing the chance to have her own little girl with Blair. She pushed that thought away quickly before she collapsed into a blubbering heap on the bed.

"This is Uncle Blair's," Holly chanted and put the bottle on the bedside table with a row of other men's toiletries before scampering off for another.

Lorna finished packing her clothes and zipped up the bag, her chest tight with suppressed emotion as she checked around the room. She fished out the small velvet box from her coat pocket and set it on top of the chest of drawers beside a silver photo frame. For a moment, she gazed at the picture of herself and Blair staring down from the top of a tree, their grinning faces side by side among the branches.

Happy days of long ago, before they had to worry about the indiscretions of their parents.

Male footsteps raced up the stairs and strode along the hall. Naomi stepped aside and Blair burst in.

"Lorna." His gaze flew from her face to the packed bag and back. "Are you leaving?"

"I thought it might be best." Her heart fluttered and dived at the sight of him, elated to have *her* Blair back instead of the withdrawn man she'd driven home, but fearful he was about to say something she didn't want to hear.

"Please don't go."

Naomi grinned. "Thank goodness." She picked Holly up, stepped out, and closed the bedroom door.

"I thought you'd need some space," Lorna said.

"Yes, I did. Sorry, love. I lost it for a while. Can we talk?" He reached out and brushed some stray hair off her forehead.

The gentle caress of his fingers on her skin elicited a shock of longing, so painful she had to bite back a gasp. She didn't want to lose Blair. Not now they'd finally found each other. She'd been fooling herself if she thought she could walk away and get on with her life as before.

She caught his hand and held on for dear life, needing the contact to reassure herself. His fingers tightened around hers. He drew her close and gathered her into his embrace. For long moments they stood together, silent, just holding each other. Blair stroked soothing circles on her back. How she loved him. If he'd rejected her, she didn't know what she'd have done.

"Forgive me for being so selfish and self-absorbed,"

he whispered.

"Of course I do. It must have been a shock." Lorna leaned back to see his face, the remorse shimmering in his blue eyes. He leaned down and kissed her forehead, the tip of her nose, and her lips.

His gaze settled on the ring box she'd put on the chest of drawers. He picked it up and weighed it in his hand. "Earlier you said that if I asked you to marry me after we'd visited your mum, then you'd agree."

Lorna nodded, excitement coiled tightly in her chest.

Blair lifted the box lid and carefully lowered himself onto one knee. He offered the ring. "Lorna Bell, will you marry me?"

Lorna had longed to be able to say yes. Earlier this afternoon, she'd thought it would never happen. Her breath hitched as she wrapped her arms around his neck. "Yes, my darling. I'd love to."

Blair rose and she spread her hand for him to slip on the ring. Pleasure zinged through her as the cool metal circled her finger, the diamond glittering in the bedroom lights.

"It's beautiful. Thank you, darling."

She fell into his arms, their lips meeting in a soft kiss. Her eyelids drifted closed as she held him tightly, vowing never to let him go. It would be awkward around his parents, but they would deal with it.

"When do you want to get married?" Blair whispered in her ear.

"As soon as possible."

"How about tomorrow?" He quirked his eyebrows.

Lorna giggled, thinking he was joking.

"I'm serious, you know."

"Serious? But tomorrow's Christmas Eve. We won't find anywhere to fit us in at such short notice."

"Duncan knows the right people. That's one of the advantages of marrying into the family of a Scottish laird."

Chapter Ten

Naomi stood back and smiled. "Oh, Lorna, the dress fits perfectly and it matches your eyes. You look wonderful."

The dove-gray silk fell just below Lorna's knees, and paired with some gray suede ankle boots looked very stylish. Naomi handed her a matching jacket. Lorna twirled around in front of the tall mirror to check the back of the outfit and gave a satisfied sigh. She'd not come prepared to be married, but Naomi had offered to lend her anything in her wardrobe.

Lorna's hair fell loose around her shoulders for once. Naomi had pinned the front back with some diamond clips that had belonged to Blair's grandmother Mackenzie.

"Knock, knock," Blair said, coming into Duncan and Naomi's bedroom. He smiled, his eyes shining with love as his gaze traveled over her. "Beautiful. I can't believe how lucky I am."

Lorna flew across the room into his arms with a squeal of joy and smothered him in kisses. "We're going to be married." She still couldn't believe it.

He laughed. "We need to hit the road in five minutes. It's a four-hour drive to Gretna Green and we need to stop on the way to buy rings."

"Four hours if we don't have any delays," Duncan added, coming up behind Blair. He'd just left Holly with Hew, who was babysitting.

Naomi grabbed her purse and kissed her husband. In a blue midi dress trimmed with Mackenzie tartan that matched Duncan's kilt, she looked stunning.

"We'll go down and get in the car," Duncan said.

"Give us a moment and we'll follow." Blair waited for his brother to leave, then returned his attention to Lorna. He raised her hand and kissed her knuckles. "I have something for you."

He pulled a small tartan rosette from his pocket. In the center was a shield decorated with the Mackenzie coat of arms. "All Mackenzie brides wear our colors and heraldic device on their wedding day."

Lorna watched as he pinned the colorful brooch to the lapel of her gray jacket. Seeing Blair attach the Mackenzie plaid and shield suddenly made this very real. She was joining his family, a noble Scottish dynasty that could trace their roots back into the mists of time.

Blair held her hands and took half a step back, a smile full of pride stretching his lips. "Lorna Mackenzie has a nice ring to it," he said softly.

Tears filled her eyes and she stepped into his arms, emotion almost overwhelming her. He'd been an important part of her life for as long as she could remember. Marrying him was so right, she couldn't imagine why it had taken them so long to do it.

"Come on, Blair." Duncan's voice sounded from below.

"Better go," Blair said.

With a tearful smile, she grabbed her purse and they hurried down the hall to join Duncan and Naomi, who were to be their witnesses at the ceremony.

Four hours later after the long car journey, Lorna read the village sign on the side of the road. "Gretna Green." She leaned forward to peer out of the car window at the low white building with a slate roof where she would tie the knot with Blair.

Never in her teenage wedding fantasies had she imagined she would be married in a blacksmith's forge. But this wasn't just any blacksmith's forge; this was a historic symbol of love that would not be denied.

Blair slipped his arm around her as he leaned across to take a look. "Gretna Green, Famous Blacksmiths Shop," he read off the large black sign at the front.

"Since 1754," Lorna added.

Duncan swung the car into the car park and pulled up. He glanced at the clock on the dashboard. "Ten minutes, everyone."

They all scrambled out. Naomi and Lorna headed to the restroom to check their hair and makeup, while the men signed in with the officials.

Fat, fluffy snowflakes started to fall as Lorna joined Blair outside the forge door.

"Ready, love?" Blair offered his arm. In his Mackenzie tartan kilt, sporran, and navy jacket with gold buttons, he was so handsome, the epitome of a noble Scottish aristocrat.

Emotion tightened Lorna's chest. She loved this wonderful man so much, she could hardly believe how lucky she was.

A piper struck up on the bagpipes and led them in through the door of the old blacksmith's forge. Sepia photographs adorned the walls, numerous horseshoes lined the wooden beams, and ancient blacksmith's tools and farming implements were arranged around the sides of the room. The rough stone walls and crooked wooden beams spoke of the centuries the building had stood here.

A jolly man, his face marked with laugh lines, waited to welcome them. Blair and Lorna stood in front of the blacksmith's anvil with Naomi and Duncan behind them as witnesses. The official welcomed them before leading them through the traditional words of the marriage ceremony.

After they exchanged rings, they rested their hands on the anvil, and the man conducting the ceremony struck the metal with a hammer.

"I now pronounce you husband and wife. You may kiss the bride."

Laughing, Lorna leaned into Blair's arms and pressed her smiling lips to his.

Duncan kissed her cheek and shook Blair's hand. "Congratulations. I'm very happy for you both."

"What a fun ceremony." Naomi hugged Lorna and Blair, laughing. "This will be something to tell the grandkids one day."

"Give us a chance." Blair chuckled. "We need to have children before we think about grandchildren."

Once they'd signed the paperwork and Blair had the wedding certificate safely tucked inside his jacket pocket, they all posed behind the anvil while one of the officials took some photos of them on Blair's phone.

Then they were guided outside by the piper playing a traditional Scottish tune. More photos were snapped of them under an arch decorated with lucky horseshoes and by the Gretna Green sign.

"Mum and Dad will be surprised when they arrive tonight," Duncan said.

"That's putting it mildly." Blair glanced at the shop that sold traditional Scottish produce. "Better buy a nice drop of local whiskey to soothe the old man."

"Hmm, I like the sound of that. Won't be a moment, love." Duncan tossed the car keys to Naomi. "Meet you back at the car in a tick."

Naomi rolled her eyes as Duncan strode off, his kilt swinging around his legs. "That man does love his whiskey," she said.

Five minutes later when they were all in the car, he returned with a big grin on his face and a carrier bag full of clinking bottles.

***

Blair cradled his wife against him as she dozed in the back of the car on the drive home. He stroked the hair off her forehead and ran his finger over her smooth skin, a sense of wonder filling his senses. Lorna was his wife, his woman to have and to hold for the rest of their lives.

This had been his dream for so many years; he couldn't remember a time when he hadn't longed to make her his. Now it was a dream no more; it was reality.

He pressed his lips to her temple as the car whizzed along the road. Passing headlights illuminated her face, giving him brief glimpses of her eyelashes resting against the curve of her cheeks, and her full lips, so soft and kissable.

How he loved her.

The revelation of the previous day still sat heavy in his thoughts, but eventually he would come to terms with what their parents had done. And he would never let it come between them again.

With that thought in mind, he considered what would happen when they arrived home. His parents were due at Kindrogan tonight. He had no idea what their reaction would be to his happy news, but he would not allow anyone to make Lorna feel unwelcome.

As they turned onto the loch road and Kindrogan Castle came into view, Lorna stirred. "Are we nearly home?"

"Five minutes. You must have smelled the air of home."

She laughed sleepily. "That was a wonderful day, but I'll be pleased to get back. I'm famished."

Naomi peered between the front seats at them. "Megan is preparing a celebratory dinner. I texted her about an hour ago to let her know when to expect us, so it should be nearly ready."

The car pulled up outside the back door. Blair wrapped his arm around Lorna as they left the warm sanctuary of the vehicle and rushed through the cold. The wonderful fragrance of roast venison greeted them as they went inside, carrying Blair back to the many celebrations at Kindrogan over the years.

"Congratulations!" Megan ran to Blair and kissed his cheek.

"Thank you, Meggie. I only hope we'll be as happy as you and Dan."

Blair released his sister, his fears at the reception Lorna would receive easing when Megan kissed and hugged her enthusiastically, then her husband, Daniel, did the same.

"Congratulations, Mrs. Mackenzie." Hew enfolded Lorna in his arms and held her tight. Blair remembered that Hew had always had a soft spot for her. He'd followed her around like a puppy when he was tiny.

"Thank you," Lorna said. "It's amazing to think you were only fifteen when I was last here. I still can't believe how you've grown up."

"Time does that to you." Hew gave her a rare smile as his son, Fergus, hugged her. Blair sometimes worried about his youngest brother. He was such a loner. He and his son needed a woman in their lives, but there seemed to be little prospect of that.

Excited by the merriment, Holly and Heather, Megan's daughter, ran around the kitchen with the dogs, shouting and clapping their hands.

"Hey, you two monkeys. Calm down." Blair sat down and caught the small giggling girls, wanting to hug them but wary of his sore abdomen.

Lorna crouched at his side and pulled Holly into her embrace. It was plain she had developed a soft spot for the wee girl. "Come here, angel, and give Auntie Lorna a kiss."

Holly placed a wet kiss on her cheek, then wriggled

to be released. Lorna grabbed pretty little red-haired Heather for a cuddle. She was small and delicate, the image of her mother, except she had her father's blue eyes.

The sound of a car outside quieted the excited conversation. Blair stood, his pulse rate increasing. He slid an arm around his wife's waist and held her to his side. She cast him a nervous glance and he offered a reassuring smile. "Nothing to worry about, love." He hoped this was true.

The back door opened and Blair's mother and father stepped inside. They paused, obviously surprised to find the kitchen full of people.

His father's gaze settled on Blair's kilt, his frown deepening. "Is this a special occasion?"

"It's Christmas Eve, Granddad," Fergus piped up. "Didn't you know?"

Everyone laughed, easing the tension in the room, but within the circle of Blair's arm, Lorna stiffened. He wasn't going to let her worry. It was time to make their announcement.

Gently, he took her left hand in his and raised it to his lips so her rings were obvious to all.

"It's very much a special occasion," he said. "We're celebrating because Lorna and I were married today."

The color drained from Sir Robert's face. He stared at Blair in shocked silence.

Blair's mother pressed a hand over her heart, her wide-eyed gaze moving from Blair to Lorna and back. "This is very sudden."

"I love Lorna. This is the happiest day of my life." Blair struggled to keep the defensive note out of his voice.

"Of course, darling. We're just surprised, that's all," Blair's mother said. "We had no idea you and Lorna were planning a wedding. Of course we're happy for you." She kissed his cheek, then turned to Lorna.

"Welcome to the family." His mother's smile seemed genuine as she embraced his new wife.

Sir Robert recovered his composure, shook Blair's hand, and then Lorna's. "My best wishes to you both."

His parents were surprised, but that was understandable. It looked as if everything would work out. The concern that had burdened Blair's thoughts fell away. If there had been a falling-out, he'd have walked away rather than make Lorna uncomfortable, but he didn't want to be estranged from his family.

"Actually, we have an announcement of our own," his father said.

Everyone's attention turned to him in expectation.

"I plan to retire and live in Barbados with your mother."

Blair caught his breath. A second chance for his parents to recapture what they'd lost and be happy again? In all his musings, this was one thing that hadn't occurred to him—and it was a wonderful outcome.

"Dad, Mum, that's fantastic news." Megan threw her arms around her parents. Blair waited for Duncan and Hew to congratulate them before he stepped forward, his throat tight with emotion, tears pricking his eyes.

He gathered his mother's slender form in his arms. "This is wonderful news. I'm so pleased. And I'm sorry for what you've been through. I only found out recently."

When he pulled back, his mother met his gaze, and a moment of understanding passed between them.

She cupped his cheek in her palm and smiled. "Thank you, darling. I appreciate that."

A cork popped as Duncan opened a bottle of champagne. Naomi lined up crystal flutes on the table while Duncan poured a splash of golden bubbly liquid into each.

The glasses were passed around and Duncan raised his. "Here's to a lifetime of happiness for Blair and

Lorna, and to a hopeful new beginning for Mum and Dad. Your very good health."

The tinkle of crystal rang out as everyone reached to tap their glasses and take a celebratory sip of champagne.

"Thank you. All of you." Blair's mother wiped away a tear as she smiled at her family, her hand resting tenderly on her husband's arm.

"We have some news as well," Duncan said. "We were going to break it tomorrow, but tonight seems to be the time for announcements... Naomi and I are going to have a baby in the summer." He placed a loving hand on his wife's abdomen.

Blair's mother gave a girlish squeal and threw her arms around Duncan and Naomi. "Wonderful news, you two."

After she'd hugged them both, she came back to Blair and rested a hand on his arm, turning a smile on Lorna. "You two don't have any similar news, do you?"

Blair spluttered into his champagne as it went down the wrong way.

An embarrassed giggle came from Lorna. "Not yet, Lady Mackenzie. We haven't had time for a honeymoon."

"Well, don't keep us waiting too long. The villa in Barbados will be empty for the next few weeks while Robert and I sort things out this end. Why don't you two spend some time over there after Christmas? It's a wonderful relaxing place for Blair to finish his recovery."

Lorna grinned at Blair, obviously pleased with the idea, and he wanted to please his new wife in every way possible, for the rest of his life. This seemed like the perfect way to start. Especially as the idea of a few lazy weeks in Barbados, just the two of them relaxing in luxury, sounded like the perfect honeymoon.

"A wonderful suggestion, Mum. Thank you."

Amidst his happy chattering family, Blair slipped his arms around Lorna and pulled her close, pressing a kiss to her lips, a sense of deep satisfaction and happiness filling him. It had taken many years, but things had worked out exactly as they should. His best friend and the love of his life wore his ring on her finger. She'd be with him for the rest of his life, and he couldn't be happier.

Epilogue

Ten months later

Vivid green tropical vegetation and jewel-bright flowers fluttered lazily in the gentle gust of the trade winds. Blair gazed across the turquoise waters of the Caribbean through eyes heavy-lidded with peace and satisfaction.

He reclined on a daybed, his darling wife curled against him, her head resting on his chest. The happy laughter and excited squeals of his extended family sounded from the swimming pool in the center courtyard of his parents' villa in Barbados, but Blair and Lorna had chosen to spend the afternoon on their private terrace outside their bedroom.

They'd had a busy morning, celebrating after his parents renewed their wedding vows in a ceremony on the beach. Life had come full circle; things that had been off-kilter had once again found their balance. All was at peace in the Mackenzie family.

The refreshing wash of air from the fan circling overhead cooled him, and Blair dozed for a few moments. He and Lorna had earned this rest and relaxation after spending the last five months treating the survivors of a hurricane, and helping care for orphaned children on a small island in the Indian Ocean.

A tiny mewling cry broke into Blair's slumber and he roused with a smile on his face. "Hey there, my wee laddie." He stretched a hand into the bassinet on the table at his side and touched the bare chest of his newborn son, Adair Robert Mackenzie, their darling little honeymoon baby.

"Is he hungry?" Lorna mumbled, stirring and leaning across Blair to peep into the baby's bed.

"I expect so." His little boy was always hungry. Unfortunately, that meant Lorna hardly got any sleep. He wished he could help with the feeding, but that was one job he couldn't do.

Lorna groaned, but she was already getting up. She circled the daybed and smiled as she gathered their tiny son, dressed only in his diaper, into her arms.

The poor little guy didn't like the heat. He wouldn't have to put up with it for much longer, though. In a few days they planned to take Adair home so he could fill his lungs with fresh Scottish air at Kindrogan Estate, and bond with his homeland.

Blair wanted his son to have all the fun he and Lorna had enjoyed as children—climbing trees, fishing in the loch, and playing in the snow.

Lorna gave birth in a hospital in Cape Town, then they'd flown on to Barbados to see his parents when Adair was three days old. Now the celebrations were over, it was time for them to go home and make plans for the future.

Lorna carried Adair back to the daybed, where Blair piled some cushions up to support her back as she lifted the hungry little boy to her breast.

Every day when Blair woke, he gave thanks for this wonderful family he'd been blessed with—his parents, his brothers and sister and their children, and most importantly, his darling wife and his amazing son.

It had taken ten years, but finally the world had righted itself. Those who loved each other had found their way back to where they belonged. Now his mother laughed like she used to, and his father had a smile on his face.

Lorna's mother had married the farmer who owned the holiday cottages where she worked, and Lorna talked to her regularly on the phone. The past would never be forgotten, but it had been laid to rest. Now they were all looking forward to the future.

Blair's happy future with Lorna and Adair was in Scotland. He'd spent many years working with children in distant parts of the world, but Scotland had its share of children in need of his care.

Lorna finished feeding their son, and Blair lifted him from her arms and rested him against his shoulder, gently patting the tiny boy's back.

Lorna leaned in and kissed him, her eyelids already drooping again. "I love you, Blair Mackenzie. You're the most wonderful man in the world. And you're a whiz at changing diapers. Not many women can say that about their husbands."

He chuckled. "Probably not something to add to my résumé." Even though working with babies and children was his vocation.

He stood up, his precious little boy cradled lovingly in his arms. The best things in life were the simplest. Nothing compared with holding his son and his darling wife in his arms, except perhaps holding a daughter in his arms.

But that was a dream for the future.

The Army Doctor's Baby

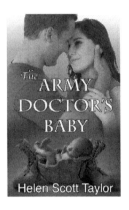

After his wife betrayed him, Major Radley Knight dedicated himself to becoming the best Army doctor he could be, dedicated himself to saving soldiers' lives. When he returns on leave from Afghanistan he is ready for a break. Instead he finds himself helping a young mother and her newborn baby. He falls in love with Olivia and her sweet baby boy and longs to spend the rest of his life caring for them. But Olivia and her baby belong to Radley's brother.

Praise for The Army Doctor's Baby

"This is a sweet romance with a wonderful happily ever after. Highly recommend this read!" Luvbooks

"I loved this sweet, tender romance about a woman in need of a father for her baby and the man who falls in love with her..." Ruth Glick

"Loved the twists at the end of the book. Just the right amount of tension to keep me turning those pages! Totally recommend." Mary Leo

The Army Doctor's Wedding

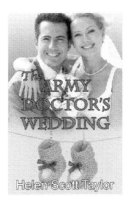

Major Cameron Knight thrives on the danger of front-line battlefield medicine. Throwing himself into saving the lives of injured servicemen keeps the demons from his past away. When he rescues charity worker, Alice Conway, and a tiny newborn baby, he longs for a second chance to do the right thing, even if it means marrying a woman he barely knows so they can take the orphan baby to England for surgery. The brave, beautiful young woman and the orphan baby steal his heart. He wants to make the marriage real, but being married to an army officer who's stationed overseas might do her more harm than good.

Praise for The Army Doctor's Wedding

"Grab a Kleenex because you are going to need it! This is one no romance lover should miss!" Teresa Hughes

"The book starts out with lots of action and holds the reader's interest through to the end. It's a great read!" Sue E. Pennington

The Army Doctor's Christmas Baby

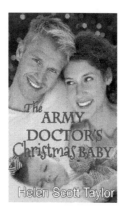

After he loses his wife, army surgeon Colonel Sean Fabian protects his damaged heart by cutting women out of his life. He dedicates himself to his career and being a great dad to his twin babies. When he asks army nurse Kelly Grace to play nanny to his children over Christmas, he realizes how much he misses having a beautiful woman in his life and in his arms. Caring for Sean's adorable twin babies is Kelly's dream come true. She falls in love with the sweet little girls and their daddy, but she's hiding a devastating event from the past. If she can't trust Sean with her secret, how can she ever expect him to trust her with his bruised heart?

Praise for The Army Doctor's Christmas Baby

"...if you want to experience the true essence of Christmas, with the love and understanding that only being with family over the holidays can satisfy, you'll definitely want to experience, The Army Doctor's Christmas Baby." F Barnett

The Army Doctor's New Year's Baby

Dr. Daniel Fabian's jet-setting lifestyle as a cosmetic surgeon to the rich and famous left him empty inside. In his quest for fulfillment he followed his brother into the army, to use his medical skills to help soldiers injured in combat. He dedicated himself to his work and cut women out of his life for twelve months. But his commanding officer's beautiful sister Megan Mackenzie is too much of a distraction for him to ignore. Amid the dangerous beauty of the Scottish Highlands, Megan rescues Daniel and shows him he's been searching in the wrong place for fulfillment. His destiny lies in her arms.

Praise for The Army Doctor's New Year's Baby

"The story is a sweet romance with a good dose of sensual tension which I enjoyed tremendously." Reader Forever

"This is a book I'd recommend to all romance lovers!" L Bird

The Army Doctor's Valentine's Baby

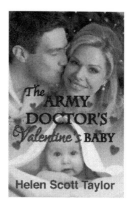

The chemistry between Captain Naomi Gray and her commanding officer, Colonel Duncan Mackenzie, sizzles, but her past means she has no use for relationships or family, and he won't date women under his command. During a week at Duncan's Scottish castle, caring for a tiny newborn baby, they fight their attraction. Can a sweet newborn who needs a mother and father bring them together?

Praise for The Army Doctor's Valentine's Baby

"This story was just perfect." Mary B

"If you haven't read this series yet then you are missing out!" Teresa Hughes

"My first book by this author and my first read of the series, it was so good I am going back to read the first four." Taina Boricua

About the Author

Helen Scott Taylor won the American Title IV contest in 2008. Her winning book, The Magic Knot, was published in 2009 to critical acclaim, received a starred review from *Booklist*, and was a *Booklist* top ten romance for 2009. Since then, she has published other novels, novellas, and short stories in both the UK and USA.

Helen lives in South West England near Plymouth in Devon between the windswept expanse of Dartmoor and the rocky Atlantic coast. As well as her wonderful long-suffering husband, she shares her home with a Westie a Shih Tzu and an aristocratic chocolate-shaded-silver-burmilla cat who rules the household with a velvet paw. She believes that deep within everyone, there's a little magic.

Find Helen at:
http://www.HelenScottTaylor.com
http://twitter.com/helenscotttaylo
http://facebook.com/helenscotttaylor
www.facebook.com/HelenScottTaylorAuthor

Book List

Paranormal/Fantasy Romance

The Magic Knot
The Phoenix Charm
The Ruby Kiss
The Feast of Beauty
Warriors of Ra
A Clockwork Fairytale
Ice Gods
Cursed Kiss

Contemporary Romance

The Army Doctor's Baby
The Army Doctor's Wedding
The Army Doctor's Christmas Baby
The Army Doctor's New Year's Baby
The Army Doctor's Valentine's Baby
Unbreak My Heart
Oceans Between Us
Finally Home
A Family for Christmas
A Christmas Family Wish
A Family Forever
Moments of Gold
Flowers on the water

Young Adult

Wildwood

Printed in Great Britain
by Amazon